The Pirate Captain's Daughter

THE PIRATE CAPTAIN'S DAUGHTER

By Eve Bunting

PUBLISHED BY SLEEPING BEAR PRESS™

Library of Congress Cataloging-in-Publication Data

The pirate captain's daughter / written by Eve Bunting.
p. cm.
Summary: Upon her mother's death, fifteen-year-old Catherine
puts her courage and strength to the test by disguising herself
as a boy to join her father, a pirate captain, on a ship whose
crew includes men who are trying to steal a treasure from him.
[1. Pirates--Fiction. 2. Seafaring life--Fiction. 3. Sex role--Fiction.
4. Fathers and daughters--Fiction.] I. Title.
PZ7.B91527Phm 2011
[Fic]--dc22
2010032409

ISBN 978-1-58536-526-5 (case)
10 9 8 7 6 5 4 3 2

ISBN 978-1-58536-525-8 (paperback)
10 9 8 7 6 5 4 3 2 1

This book was typeset in Adobe Caslon Pro and ITC Blackadder
Cover design by Richard Tuschman

Printed in the United States.

Sleeping Bear Press™

315 East Eisenhower Parkway, Suite 200
Ann Arbor, Michigan 48108

© 2011 Sleeping Bear Press is an imprint of Gale, a part of Cengage Learning.

visit us at www.sleepingbearpress.com

Printed by Bang Printing, Brainerd, MN, 2ⁿᵈ Ptg., 05/2011

To my friends, the writers of lunch bunch

Chapter One

I always knew my father was a pirate and I always knew I wanted to be one, too. But I had to stay home to look after my mother, who was sickly. And besides, I was a girl and maybe at fifteen a bit young, though of course I didn't think so.

I suspected my mother also knew my father was a pirate but she pretended to herself and to me that he was still a captain in the Royal Navy. My mother was a proper Boston lady of Scottish ancestry, accustomed to the theater and the opera before she met and fell in love with her dashing naval man—a dashing naval man who'd turned out to be something different.

I didn't suppose he'd ever revealed to her that he and the whole crew had mutinied and that they'd taken over the naval ship and become pirates. They'd found that their three-masted square-rigger was not maneuverable enough and they'd soon spotted a two-masted schooner, attacked it, and taken it over. They renamed her *Reprisal* and exchanged the mermaid on her bowsprit for a dragon figurehead, more in keeping with their new line of business.

How did I know all this? I'd heard my father and his quartermaster, Mr. Trimble, talking in our parlor when I was supposed to be in the kitchen preparing food. Mr. Trimble had a lady friend who also lived in Port Teresa and so he and my father came here together when the *Reprisal* was careened in Cannon Cove for repairs, out of sight of the town.

I added to my knowledge of my father's life by eavesdropping each time they talked and by reading between the lines. I have a talent for both these enterprises. One night I heard my father say, "Maggie knows where it is. She can find it when it's necessary." Maggie is my mother.

"Is it safe?" Mr. Trimble had asked. "There are those who'd have it at any price. Even her life."

"It's safe," my father said in a tone that allowed of no further questions.

I'd slipped away, wondering. What was "it"? Who were "those" people Mr. Trimble was talking about?

⚓

My father and Mr. Trimble came today—two jaunty, well-dressed gentlemen, each walking with a swagger, not because they're proud but because that's the way seafaring men walk to keep their balance on the heaving deck of a sailing ship. They were never in naval uniform. My father had explained to my mother that they liked to leave their uniforms behind on the *Reprisal*. I decided for myself that those naval uniforms had probably been tossed overboard a long while ago.

My father always wore fine garments, which I presumed he had taken from some rich man on a plundered merchant ship. Today his trousers were of black velvet, his coat and stockings were scarlet silk, and his coat embroidered with silver. He didn't wear a wig and I was pleased about that. He has such a head of curling black hair, which he ties in back in a braid.

My mother, as usual, was poorly this day. She had taken to her bed the month before and my father looked serious when he came down from sitting with her. He had been with her for a long time, during which Mr. Trimble and I had little to say to one another.

"Is your lady worse, Cap'n?" Mr. Trimble asked when my father reappeared.

"Aye. The pneumonia has taken her strength. The good doctor Pugliese is not encouraging." My father sighed. "I fear…" he stopped as if suddenly aware of me. His voice changed to what I decided was a false cheerfulness. "Catherine, girl! Fetch Mr. Trimble and me some of that elderberry wine your mother made."

"I'm beginning to have a taste for your good wife's wine," Mr. Trimble said. "It's near as good as a tot of strong Madagascar rum. I reckon it'll do till we get something better."

I thought that was quite rude of Mr. Trimble since he had two or three glasses each time he came. I went in the pantry to fetch the bottle.

Mr. Trimble drank his usual three glasses and then took his leave to go visit his ladylove. My father and I sat in the parlor and talked. He's always been loving to me, tender and respectful of my mother, interesting in his tales of where he's been and the sights he's seen but vague about details. Did he know I guessed his true vocation? If he did he never confirmed it.

Today, just before he was to leave to go back to his ship, he told me, "I'll be gone for three months or more,

Catherine. We sail in two days. I'm loath to put the burden of your mother's health on you but there's no one else to help. Unless we ask your great aunt Louise if she'd be kind enough to come from Boston..."

"I can manage," I told my father quickly. I'd met my great aunt Louise once. She was not at all like my mother, being bossy and prim and prone to sniffing if she didn't agree with you.

"You know how to reach old Bunty Bosun?" he asked. "Bunty can always get word to me. He knows every ship that sails in and out of this harbor." He half smiled. "And the ones that stay clear of the harbor, too."

I knew where to find Bunty. Bunty had been a pirate himself. That was understood. He sat every day on a bench at the dock, barefoot, smoking his pipe, his parrot, Swabbie, on the bench beside him. Bunty couldn't talk, having lost his tongue long ago. My father never explained how that had happened and I didn't want to know. Swabbie did the talking for him. "Avast, me hearties, I'll tell ye a tale," he'd croak in his old man's voice, and he had some sailor words too that scandalized the ladies passing by. Neither Bunty nor Swabbie had ever sailed on the *Reprisal* but I knew my father gave them money. It was Bunty who came to the house once every month and silently handed over the little packets of powder that helped my mother sleep and stilled her cough. I blessed him, just as silently.

My father was leaving.

"Take care of your mother," he said. He took my face in his hands, hands that were rough and calloused. A pirate's hands that had known ropes and sails and scrubbers. I felt his light kiss on the top of my head.

"*You* take care, Father," I whispered and I watched him go, striding down the hill, his black curly pigtail swinging against the back of his scarlet coat. How I longed to go with him, to whatever new adventure the *Reprisal* was headed for.

I'd never seen my father's ship except in my imagination. Now I imagined her slicing through the blue waters of the Caribbean, her sails like fat white geese, the sky scudding by. I heard the lookout in the crow's nest, shouting, "A sail! A sail!" and I saw the plump, unsuspecting merchant ship coming over the horizon and *Reprisal*'s innocent flag skittering down the mast, the Jolly Roger taking its place. It would snap in the wind and *Reprisal* would lean over, eager to seize and plunder. I visualized the merchant ship surrendering as soon as she saw that pirate flag. There were tales of brutality and bloodshed in pirate attacks. I'd heard them. But I knew that would not be the way of the *Reprisal*. My father was a kindly man. I'd seen the way he was with my mother, how he'd brush her hair, freeing it from its tangle on the pillow, how he'd read to her, hour after hour, his face so gentle in the candle's light. I remembered the time our long-ago cat, Timothy, had been taken ill and how my father had been the one to care for him, to hand-feed him tidbits of fish. It was difficult for me to believe my father could be cruel. But perhaps he changed when he got on board his ship. Perhaps he had to.

I watched him walk down the hill till he was out of sight, then I went back inside and closed the door on adventure and excitement. When my father left it seemed the shine went out of the world.

That night, after I'd tended to my mother, sponged her dear hands and face and brought her usual cup of warm milk I went early to bed. For a while I read *The Adventures of Robinson Crusoe*, a new book that had great appeal to me since it was based on a true story. I blew out my candle and dreamed one of my half-awake dreams about pirate ships, and desert islands filled with strange animals. I wasn't sure if I was awake or asleep when I heard a noise. It came from downstairs and it was so faint that for a minute I thought I had imagined it and lay back on my pillows. But there it was again. A door opening so gently, or a drawer perhaps. My first thought was that my mother had wakened and somehow stumbled downstairs. How could she? She was so weak that she could hardly get out of her bed without help.

My father? Come back, afraid to alarm us, coming in silent as a ghost? I had to know.

I slipped out of bed and to the landing outside my room. The dark was all around me. The only sound was the roughness of my breath. And then I heard the footfalls, spaced apart, pausing often as if afraid of being heard.

Whoever it was, they were coming up the stairs. I flattened myself against the wall, glad that the nightgown Aunt Louise had sent was a rather ugly shade of gray. My heart beat furiously against my chest. It had to be my father. I should pounce and scare him as he had scared me. But something stopped me, some built-in alarm. It was too dark for even a shadow but I knew the presence in my house was not my father.

Chapter Two

The air was charged along the landing. Where was the man going? What was that sound? I tensed, listening with every sense. The noise was a small grinding. He was opening the door to my mother's room. My father had said the hinge had need of oil and he'd see to it on his next visit home.

No!

I sprang forward screaming, waving my arms, shouting, "Get away. Go!"

I heard a gasp and I bumped into a figure, still unseen, in front of me. I was against a chest or a stomach, rough cloth under my face, a smell of something sickeningly sweet, like the scent of the gardenias that grew in my mother's garden. And then I was thrown back against the wall. A hoarse voice muttered something and there was the drum of heavy feet running toward the stairs. I lay against the wall, half stunned, a strange whining sound in my ears and through it my mother's weak voice calling, "Catherine? Catherine? Is that you? What is happening?"

I pulled myself up, my palms flat against the wall. Her door was slightly open where he'd turned the knob. I spoke softly. "I was coming, Mother. I thought I heard you call. I tripped. Wait just a minute." I ran to the window at the top of the stairs and peered down at the street below. There was no one there. Bushes moved at the edge of our garden. Was someone hiding behind them? Where did he go? I strained, alert for any disturbance outside. There was nothing except the call of a night bird high in the Greenheart tree.

"Catherine?" I heard my mother's pitiful voice and that cough that tore through her chest and brought an ugly flush to her face.

"I'm coming." I was aware that my left elbow ached. I hurried to my mother's bedside.

"I was careless," I said. "I should have brought a light so I could see. Are you all right?"

My hands trembled as I held the match to the candle

on her dresser.

"Do you need anything?"

I helped her swallow a few sips of water and mixed up one of the small packets of powder to leave by her bedside should she not sleep again.

"I don't think I called you, Catherine. But sometimes now I'm not sure what is real and what is dream. I was dreaming you and I and your father were gathering shells on Bell Beach. Perhaps I did call out for you."

"Can you sleep again now?" I asked and I smoothed back her hair. "Shall I blow out your candle?"

"Yes. You know you are the dearest daughter anyone ever had?" she asked and smiled her weak smile.

I didn't know it then, but they were the last words she would ever speak to me. If I'd known, I would have sat with her so she would not be alone as she drifted into the forever darkness. But I didn't know.

Before I went back to my own bed I lit the lantern we kept by the stairs and went around our house, making sure all was locked. I found where the intruder had entered. A pantry window, half opened to the air, had been jammed to its fullest width. There was soft dirt or sand on the sill. I snibbed it tight.

I didn't get into bed right away. All my senses were wide awake. I decided that tomorrow I would go and find old Bunty and have my father come at once. He would know what we should do. I lay rigid in my bed wondering if this was one of the "they" my father had spoken of. One of the "they" who had come searching for "it," whatever "it" was.

I'd send that message with Bunty Bosun early in the morning. I did send it but it was not the one I had decided on. It was the worst message in the world, that my mother had died in her sleep that night.

Bunty crossed himself and then, using his own means, whatever they were, he got the word to my father.

My father came back that afternoon and together we made plans for my mother's funeral. I told him too about the strange happening of last night. "He was going in my mother's room," I whispered.

My father made a small, startled sound. "Here? Someone came here?" There was a moment's pause. His face was tight and angry. The way he emphasized "someone" made me suspect that my father knew who it was who'd entered our house in the dark of night. But then he said in a lighter voice that I knew immediately to be designed to mislead me, "There are men who hang around the harbor, men who are not above robbing and stealing. You must have been frightened."

"I was." I didn't challenge him. Very soon I'd be needing

his good will and support. If my plan worked there would be time later to ask him questions.

At the gravesite next day we clung together and I quieted my sobs against his chest. My mother was buried in the little cemetery at the top of Cob Hill free of her suffering at last. Mr. Trimble came, and Bunty and Swabbie and a scattering of townspeople. Mr. Mulligan who had the shop on Main Street and sold us our provisions every week, Miss Swarton who has been my pianoforte and flute teacher since I was five years old, Mr. Crabtree who tended my mother's garden after she got too ill to tend it herself. We didn't know too many of the island people, my mother always being one who favored keeping to ourselves. Swabbie was mercifully quiet.

My father had suggested I play my flute at the burial. "That piece you composed yourself, the one your mother liked so much," he said.

I nodded. And standing there on Cob Hill beside her newly turned grave I played the part of the melody where my mother said she could hear stars spinning and bears dancing and rain falling silver on silver leaves. I felt as if my heart was breaking.

As we were leaving my father placed a piece of pink coral on the lid of the coffin and murmured words I couldn't hear. He wiped tears from his eyes. Then we left, leaving my mother behind. I looked back and I thought that lonely coffin waiting there was the saddest thing I'd ever seen.

The headstone was ordered the next day. Together my father and I chose the words that would be chiseled into it:

ELIZA DeVAULT,
BELOVED WIFE AND MOTHER
LET LOVE CLASP GRIEF
LEST BOTH BE DROWNED

The line came from one of my mother's favorite poems by Alfred Lord Tennyson.

"I will think of this, and her, and the place where she lies," my father said as we left the stonemason's and he wiped his eyes with his handkerchief.

We walked in silence.

At last he spoke.

"I have asked Miss Swarton if she will come and stay with you nights while I'm gone," he said when we were back home. "I have made provisions to have double locks placed on all the doors and windows. Still, you cannot be alone. When I return we will make lasting arrangements for you." He took my hands. "Catherine, it hurts me to leave you like this, but go I must." He seemed about to say more but stopped. "Today I will pen a letter to your aunt Louise. It might be more agreeable for you to go to her in Boston."

We were sitting side by side on the settle in the parlor, the shutters closed against the sunlight in respect of my mother's death. My elbow still ached and I rubbed it as if warming myself as I stood to face him.

"I am going, too," I said. "I'm going to be a pirate. Like you," I added.

I saw the shock in his eyes. "You know that I am a pirate?"

"I'm not a child. I have known for a long time. You can let me sail with you on the *Reprisal,*" I went on, for I'd thought it all through. "Else I'll find myself another ship. I would be safer with you, but if you won't have me, a different captain will."

My father's voice seemed to have left him.

I stood, my shaking hands clasped behind me.

"So which will it be?" I asked. "I'm not staying here. Even with double locks. Miss Swarton and I could both be in danger and that would certainly be unfair to her. And now that Mother's gone." My voice broke. Now that Mother's gone sounded like a requiem. "I'm not having Aunt Louise come and I'm not going to her. We would drive one another mad. Will you take me? Or do I fend for myself?" I spoke strongly, not betraying the tremble inside of me.

He stood too.

"My," he said mildly. "Such big words from such a small person."

He touched my cheek. "Ah, but you can't come with me, Catherine, or go with another captain. A girl..."

I interrupted. "No one will know that I am a girl. I can make myself look like a boy. And I'm not a small person. I am tall, above average in height for a girl. But if you're so concerned, remember, I'd be safer with you as my captain." I paused for breath. "I swear I'll run away. With you or without you, I will be a pirate."

Chapter Three

My father and I talked almost till dawn. Our talk was of my conviction that I could do this, my assurances that I would do it, whatever his decision, interspersed with reminiscences of my mother, weeping and memories. Now and then some recollection brought a smile, or even a laugh.

There was no mention of the night's intruder.

I used every power of persuasion of which I was capable to convince my father to allow me to come with him. "For at least this one voyage," I said. "You said it would be only three months long." And I added: "I have no mother now, and I need to be with you."

That was indeed true. I felt guilty though when my

words made his tears well up again and I knew I was using unfair means to convince him.

"Very well," he said at last. "You will come with me. Provided you can do what you say and make yourself less like my daughter and more like my son. And I must have your assurance that you will never, ever, reveal that you are a girl. You cannot know what terrible danger there would be, for us both, if it were discovered I have brought a daughter and not a son."

I nodded.

"And you must never expect more attention from me than I give my crew. Once we are aboard we will be as strangers. It will be safer that way."

"I understand."

For a moment he held me tight. I whispered against his shoulder. "I promise that I will never expect favors or kindly regard from you. I will be a true pirate."

Eventually we retired.

The house was filled with my mother's presence, her books, her paintings. I was comforted to have my father there, but still, I wakened often, listening for a sound. I roused several times, missing my mother's cough, thinking I heard her calling for me, even getting out of bed once to remember with desolation that she would never call out for me again.

My father had contacted Miss Swarton and told her I would be going away for a while and we would no longer need her services. He gave Mr. Crabtree some silver pieces and asked him to come tend to our garden as usual, even though we'd be gone.

⚓

I cut my hair, hacking at it with my mother's small sewing scissors. It fell to the floor of the kitchen in black clumps that shifted in the air that came under the door. They looked like small, furry animals slithering laboriously about. My mother had called my hair my "crowning glory" and she would have hated to see me cut it but I felt no loss. This was the first part of the plan.

My father went into town and bought clothes for me, the kind of clothes I had never worn in my lifetime. In my room I discarded my dress, my chemise, my petticoat, bloomers, and stockings. I put on the ankle-length canvas trousers, the loose black-and-white striped shirt that was too big and the laced-up canvas shoes, which were too small and already hurt my toes. But I would not complain. There was a red scarf to tie around my head.

I could hear my father pacing in the parlor. I could hear his footsteps and I imagined his impatience to be off.

His ship was likely ready by now. Our ship.

He took one look at me when I entered the room, nodded and said, "Let me see. Yes. You will pass if you are careful and put away your girlish mannerisms."

He smiled when I objected.

"I do not have girlish mannerisms."

He tapped his teeth with a forefinger. "What name shall we give you, then? Charlie, I think. It is close enough to Catherine so you will remember to answer to it."

"Charlie," I repeated. And I think it was at that moment that I realized I had taken a step into something strange and new. It was the step I wanted with all my heart but still, the unknown is frightening.

We walked around our house, going from room to room, bolting doors, shuttering and locking windows. I took extra care with the one in the pantry. I had a strong sense that this intruder had been searching for "it" that he suspected was here. Was he off the *Reprisal*? I remembered the strange feeling I'd had that my father knew who he was.

"We'll be back," my father said, likely seeing my shiver and thinking I was in need of comfort. "This voyage is short. After that, who knows? I would have it in my heart to postpone it but the men are ready and so is the ship. I have no choice."

I took only one thing with me, my flute. I stood in my

mother's room, looking around at all the familiar things. The jar of shells and sea rocks and glass that we'd gathered on Bell Beach. The small locket that held her picture and the baby one of me. A boy would never take such things and it might be difficult to keep them hidden. I kissed her picture and returned the locket to my treasure box.

We bolted the doors behind us and left without looking back. How easily we'd abandoned our old lives.

Joshua Cunningham has a horse and carriage for hire at the edge of town. To be true about it, the carriage is really a cart that rattles and bumps as it rolls along the rough roads. My bones rattled with it.

He drove us to Cannon Cove and I knew by the talk between them that my father used his services each time he came to the island.

"I see ye have a new boy to go sailing wi' ye," Joshua said. "A musician by the looks of the flute he be carryin'."

"Aye," my father said. "He has a desire for the sailing life and begged to go."

Joshua Cunningham cackled. "I reckon he'll find it more than he bargained for." His grin showed rotted-out teeth. "I been hearin' you got musicians that plays on your ship, Cap'n."

My father only nodded and I stayed quiet. Least said the better.

We were left off at a distance from Cannon Cove and tramped the rest of the way, my father going ahead, me hobbling behind in my too-tight shoes. His scarlet coat swayed as he walked and I caught a glimpse of the broad-bladed cutlass that was tucked in his waist sash. It didn't worry me. A cutlass would be part of a pirate's rig and though I'd never seen him wear it in our house I'd often watched him slip it into place when he left to go back to his ship.

Our path ran along the cliff top above the ocean, which shimmered blue and empty into the distance. Brambles clawed at my bare ankles. Once a golden butterfly flew down to land on my shoulder. I felt it like a blessing and I decided to consider it so.

It was a strange and lovely feeling to be out here in the air and sunshine, unencumbered by skirt and chemise. I felt my sorrow lifting and then I thought of the night intruder, shadowy and unreal. If he had come off the *Reprisal* and was still on board, my father would see to him. I wasn't alone.

If only my shoes didn't hurt my toes! I limped along, not wanting to complain. My father might consider that a girlish mannerism.

After a time he seemed to notice my hobbling walk.

"Too small?" he asked, lifting up one of my feet.

I tottered and held on to his arm.

"We'll fix that," he said, and before I knew what was happening he'd pulled off my shoe, whipped out his cutlass and sliced off the canvas top down by the toe so that there was only the sole and half of the upper left. I felt the swish of air as the cutlass carved through the air.

"I'm glad your aim is good," I muttered, and my father smiled.

"It has had practice. Give me the other shoe."

In a minute he had done surgery on it too.

"Better," I said, wiggling my toes and I felt such a wave of happiness swiftly followed by guilt. How could I feel happy when my mother had just died? I was a monster.

We turned a bend in the path and were all at once looking down on Cannon Cove. And there was the *Reprisal* careened on the sand. But even helpless, she had a beauty about her. My breath caught in my throat and I was filled with happiness again.

The ship's cannons had been pulled high, away from the tide and they lay shining in the sun, deadly even in their silence. Now I could see that her tall masts were tied to the tops of the trees that grew down to the sand. Tied like that the crew had been able to tip her over with less damage. The blocks and tackles that had been used lay close to her.

Men swarmed around her, clambered over her sides and on her decks.

I knew about careening. It had to be done every few months to clean the ship's hull of teredo worms and make any necessary repairs under the water line.

I smelled tar and creosote and the putrid stink of the rotting sea life that lay, scraped from her bottom. Shouts and curses and loud laughter competed with the sounds of saws and hammers. There was music, too, coming from somewhere. I took a deep breath. I could never have imagined such a scene.

Standing apart from the others was Mr. Trimble, the quartermaster. I stepped closer to my father. "Mr. Trimble will recognize me."

"Don't worry about Mr. Trimble," my father said. "I'll see to it that he keeps our secret. I have kept others of his." He shaded his eyes from the sun. "She's just about ready to be pulled back in the water, Charlie. We're in good time."

I looked to see whom he was addressing, then understood.

My life as Charlie had begun.

Chapter Four

The musicians stopped playing, the men stopped singing and working as my father and I scrambled down the path.

Mr. Trimble looked at me, raised one eyebrow but said nothing. I suspected he already understood that this was to be another secret shared with my father.

My father introduced me to the crew in a voice I hadn't heard before.

"Avast, mateys. This here is my son. His mother died and I'm taking him with me." He spoke in the way I thought a pirate captain would speak, stern, and definite. I was proud of his air of authority.

There were some mumblings and before there could be more said my father added: "There'll be no favors asked and none given, you may lay to that! His name is Charlie. He is twelve years old."

I gulped. Twelve? In truth I was fifteen. Why had he changed my age?

"But Cap'n. We have us a cabin boy, and a good un," someone shouted. "We got no need for another."

My father turned to me and hoisted my shirt up a mite above my waistband, gesturing toward the flute I'd tucked in the top of my trousers. I put my arms across my body. What was he doing? A few inches more and it would have been apparent I wasn't a boy—and that I was older than twelve. My father had forgotten that as a young woman I had bosoms, concealed well by the loose-fitting shirt he had bought for me but obvious if he had pulled that shirt a little higher. Under the gaze of the men I felt my face grow hot at the thought. How was I going to keep my true self a secret from these men? And if they found out, what then? I'd heard how disastrous a violation of conduct could be when I'd been eavesdropping once on a conversation my father had with Mr. Trimble. I'd missed the beginning of it.

"If the men ever get wind of this, they'll have your hide," Mr. Trimble had said. "They voted you to be captain and they can vote you out just as readily."

"Aye," my father had answered. "It's the curse of true democracy." His tone was light, almost mocking.

"We don't want to think on what they might do to you," Mr. Trimble said seriously, and they had fallen into a deep silence. I'd hurried away, wondering what my father had done in the past that I didn't know about. They couldn't find out about me, I thought now. I'd have to be watchful every minute.

My father was speaking again. "My son is a musician. He will join the ship's band."

"No offense, Cap'n. A boy of twelve can't play no music that would please us." That was a little fellow, brown as a nut, holding a hammer that he smashed against his arm as he spoke.

Another man, one with a patch over his right eye, began singing an old nursery rhyme in a tone dripping mockery.

"Mary had a little lamb
Its fleece was white as snow."

There was a roar of derisive laughter.

I thrust the parcel I carried at my father, pulled out the flute and strode toward the two men who had been playing the instruments. They stood to the side of the *Reprisal,* their feet planted in the hard sand. One had an accordion, a squeezebox as we used to call it. I didn't let myself stare at his shining wooden leg or the crutch that lay on the sand next to him. The second man had a fiddle.

I took a deep breath, moistened the mouthpiece of the flute and also my own lips that had gone suddenly dry with apprehension. I would play and I would surprise them all. I would surprise myself.

I began on a sea shanty I'd heard my father sing at home to my mother, a rollicking, happy tune that had always made her smile. I knew it well.

My wiggling toes moved in their own independent dance, sand sifting up scratchy between them as I played the tune over.

They were listening, joining in on the chorus.

At the end of two verses my father raised his arm. "All right. No more slacking, lads. Back to work. We want her ready to float with the tide." And to me, in just as rough a way he said, "Get along then, and make some music with the men."

I moved to be beside the fiddler. As the two of them started to play I joined in. It was another shanty, one I'd never heard of, but I had enough music in me to be able to keep pace, even if it was more of a tootledy-toot than a tune. Miss Swarton, my pianoforte and flute teacher, would have frowned.

While we played, the men sang and worked, hauling on lines, hammering what I thought were the last of the nails, rolling barrels of water down the slope of the sand, hauling boxes of oranges and lemons.

I felt the other musicians glancing at me and away again in case I'd catch them looking. I examined them, too. The accordion player was old enough to be a grandfather. His wooden leg was buried up to where the knee would have been and he had a surly, angry look about him in spite of the mirthful music he coaxed from his squeezebox. Now and then he spat into the sand. Because of his half-buried stump he had to stand lopsided and I wondered how he would be able to walk in that damp sand even with the help of the crutch. The second man was small and fat with sparse ginger whiskers. He wore a three-cornered black hat and there were ginger hairs on his belly that bulged over the tops of his knee-length trousers like an air-filled balloon. His bare feet thumped in time to the music.

The tide crept up the beach. Soon it lapped around my ankles, then my knees. The crutch was now under the arm of its owner to save it from floating away.

And still we played.

I tried to count how many pirates there were, milling around on the beach and clambering over the *Reprisal* but it was hard to tell. Perhaps thirty. They were nimble and strong, each one with a knife stuck in the top of his droopy trousers. I had identified one as probably the cabin boy. He was about my age, my real age and he had yellow hair that shone in the sun.

Sometimes I got a glimpse of my father or Mr. Trimble urging along a lazy pirate. There was much shouting and loud talk. I knew I'd have to get used to the coarseness of the words if I was to live among these men. But I promised my mother again I'd never use that language myself.

From time to time, one or another of the men would disappear into the bushes. I had no trouble guessing what he was doing there and I knew I needed to disappear from view soon myself. I took the opportunity when we stopped for a quiet spell to slip away. It was only then that I began having worries and indelicate wonderings that I hadn't faced when I'd imagined myself a pirate. What kind of commodes would they have on the *Reprisal?* Would there be somewhere to withdraw to alone, I wondered.

Waves had covered the keel now and licked up the side of the beached ship. My father was calling out. "All hands to the task. Make ready to set her afloat."

"See lad, we have to move her at just the right time, not a minute before and not a minute after. We have to catch her when the tide's full in and deep enough to lift her." It was the small fat man talking to me quite cheerfully. We stood to one side, watching as the men used their block and tackle to help the *Reprisal* rise to an upright position. The ropes that held the masts to the tops of the trees were finally untied. She had been beached stern in and now a few men clambered on board her. Six others pushed the rowboat off the sand and jumped in. With a few strong strokes they pulled away from the beach. A rope thrown from the *Reprisal* sizzled through the air and landed in the water. One of the six retrieved it and fastened it to the stern of their rowboat. As they bent their backs to the oars the *Reprisal* came slowly behind them into the deeper water of the bay.

Oh, how pretty she looked with her black paint and her golden scrollwork. The red dragon figurehead seemed to snort and pant, its eyes fixed on the far horizon. I felt a swell of pride. My ship!

The men in the rowboat continued to pull on her and she came with them.

"But how can they move her?" I asked, amazed. "She's so big!"

"She be floating, that's how, lad," the red-haired fellow told me.

"And the tide's pulling her nicely, too." He turned to face me. "You play a fine whistle, Charlie. We'll be glad of you. So you will know, they call me Red."

"Thanks, Red," I said, pleased.

The one-legged man glared at me balefully but didn't offer his name. I nodded in as friendly a way as I could manage.

"Jump for the ropes, the rest of you lubbers," someone shouted and the men who were left on the beach splashed into the water leaping for the ropes that hung over the *Reprisal*'s sides. Now what was I seeing? A giant of a man, his bare chest a mat of black hair, came over to where we stood. Effortlessly he hoisted the squeezebox musician onto his back and I saw that it, too, was thick with black hair. The accordion player had his instrument under one of his arms, his crutch under the other as they hauled themselves aboard the ship.

"Stop gawking, laddie boy," Red said. "They be brothers and two of a kind." He didn't make the words sound like a compliment. "Herc and Hopper McDonald. Keep out of their way if ye wants to survive aboard ship." He gave me a push. "Time to go, matey."

I nodded, tucked my flute back in the top of my canvas trousers and splashed waist deep into the water. I caught hold of a dangling rope and began pulling myself up. It wasn't easy. Not for me, though I saw others swarming aboard like monkeys. The rope burned my hands, the ship rocked unsteadily. I clawed up the sides of the *Reprisal* with my toes that stuck out from my half shoes, searching for a foothold. My nose was filled with the smell of paint and tar. Up, up. My elbow ached where the man who'd broken into our house, the night man, had pushed me against the wall.

I could reach the gunwales now. Somehow I had to heave myself over the top and onto the deck.

Above me, on board, Mr. Trimble was shouting. I had no trouble knowing his voice.

"Help the lad up. Grab a hold of his hands."

And somebody was stretching down, dragging me roughly aboard.

I was yanked so hard my arms felt like they were coming out of their sockets. I was against a furry, wet chest and I stumbled back and looked up into the face of the big man, the one who'd carried the accordion player. Herc or Hopper, likely Herc I thought.

"Thank ye," I gasped.

"You'll need to do better if ye're to be part of this crew, Cap'n's son or not," the man said. There was an ugly sneer in his voice and I smelled him, smelled that sickening, unmistakable scent. Although it was mixed now with rancid sweat I recognized it immediately.

It was him.

Chapter Five

I stood on the deck of the *Reprisal,* dazed and confused. Herc was the man who'd broken into our house. He was off the *Reprisal* and he'd been looking for something. I knew instantly that he'd been searching for "it." Somehow he knew or suspected "it" was in our house.

He hadn't succeeded. I had stopped him. Now he was staring down at me. Was there any way he could have seen me clearly in that scuffle outside my mother's room? Could he have known I was a girl? I doubted it. The dark had been close around us and I must have been only a shadow in my gray nightgown. He was looking at me now, and I felt sure he was thinking, this boy, this hopeless-looking boy in his broken shoes was the one who stopped me last night. The captain's son. But he wouldn't know I had recognized him. With one last look he strode away. I took a shuddering breath.

I must tell my father about him, and quickly.

I looked along the deck of the ship. Oh blessed glory! I was here!

But... this couldn't be the *Reprisal*, the beautiful, sleek, shining ship of my dreams. The deck was dirty beyond anything I had ever seen. It was black with spilled oil, grease, and grime. Everywhere were jumbles of tarred ropes, mildewed sails, anchors with weed and dead fish clinging to them, everything crowded together where they had slid when the ship was careened.

Had the crew just attended to the outside hull? It seemed that way.

There was chaos and confusion all around me as the pirates hauled on ropes and sails and crates. Barrels rolled this way and that with the slight sway of the ship, even though we were anchored. There were shouts and curses and other sounds I couldn't identify. They seemed to be the frightened cluckings of chickens. They had chickens on board? Yes. Two limp-looking hens fluttered past me, scattering their droppings as they went and a small, brown pirate raced behind, ignoring the birds, collecting the droppings on his bare feet.

"Down below with ye," he shouted. "Ye got out of your cages, ye varmints. I've a mind to wring yer necks right now afore yer time." He scooped them up by their feet and disappeared down some steps.

Another pirate rolled a cask in my direction. He had a blue kerchief around his neck and he stopped, jerked it from his neck, honked into it, then replaced it at his throat.

I kept pace with him as the cask rolled. How to phrase this unseemly but essential question?

"I need to pee. Where may I do that?"

"Ye need to pee? Stand on the leeward channel, lad, and do it over the side. Make certain the wind is blowing away from ye."

I ran along beside him. My shoes oozed water. My wet trousers flapped against my legs. Scrapes and cuts stung. I panted out the words. "I need to do more than that."

He stopped the cask, keeping it from rolling by placing a bare foot on top of it. "More than pee?" This time he laughed out loud. "By heaven you're a timid whelp! Up at the bow, boy. Ye'll find two seats of easement. What you do drops in the bay."

"Thank ye," I said.

I hurried through the confusion on the deck, tripping

over ropes and almost bumping into two goats that were wandering amongst the men working. I saw the yellow-haired cabin boy, coiling a rope that was thick as my arm.

I had reached the bow of the ship now. A wooden structure hung below it. There were two boxes on it, each with a hole cut on top. I climbed down. Each one had a hole in the bottom too, and bending over I could see, through the opening, the blue water of the bay. All was quiet. There was just me and the red dragon jutting out above. I hurried before I would be seen.

I was making my way back along the deck, much relieved by my visit to the seat of easement when someone said, "Boy!"

I stopped.

"Cap'n wants you in his cabin."

I looked around and saw the accordion player, Hopper. He thumped on the deck with his wooden leg, glaring at me, slit-eyed, waving his crutch toward the other side of the ship. Did he know about "it" and his brother's encounter with me?

"Where is the Cap'n's cabin?"

"Are ye stupid, boy? Am I not showing ye? Starboard, 'tween decks."

I made a move to go when the crook of his crutch caught around my arm, staying me. "We be playing our music every day of the week, every hour of the day, 'cept on the Sabbath. An' we don't hold with slackers. Ye heed when I calls ye."

"Aye," I mumbled, and the crutch eased its grip on me. I hurried away.

Below, in the bay, I heard the sounds of a rowboat, oars dripping water, men's voices, and I took a glance over the side of the ship. The rowboat had gone ashore and was ferrying the boxes of fruit I'd seen and barrels of water to the ship.

'Tween decks the one-legged man had said. Starboard? I picked my steps again through spare masts, sails, crudely folded hen droppings, and goat dirt.

I don't know how I expected a captain's cabin to be, but this was not it. Nothing thus far had been as I had imagined. The cabin door was open. I saw my father, his back to me, sitting at a desk that was no more than a plank littered with papers and charts. It was held up by the stumps of two tree trunks. There was a small bed, a long cupboard, a dresser, if you could call it that. On it was a tortoise-shell brush and the matching comb with a silver band across the top. My mother had given him those. They were the only civilized objects in the room and the sight of them brought tears to my eyes. I wiped them away. Pirates don't cry, I told myself.

My father no longer wore his fancy breeches and scarlet coat. Instead he had on loose canvas trousers, cut off below the knee, a white shirt with balloon sleeves and a red waistcoat. Under the desk his feet were bare.

I stared at them for a minute. I didn't believe I'd ever seen my father's feet.

A small stained mirror hung above the dresser and on some pegs drooped a few articles of ordinary clothing, like the other pirates wore.

I coughed to let him know I was here and he stood up.

"I see you found your way aboard all right," he said, and it was my own dear father's voice, my own dear father's warm smile. "You did well. I watched you. But you understand I cannot single you out for any special treatment?"

"I understand."

"So come you in. I would ask you to close the door, but the door of a captain's cabin is never closed. The men come and leave as they please."

"Oh," I said. And I remembered how my father had described it—the curse of pirate democracy.

"Look here." My father strode to a bundle in a corner, unrolled it and I saw it was a canvas hammock. "You will sleep here," he said. "It will be safe for you and easily explained to the men. There is no room anywhere on board the *Reprisal* for another hammock to swing. I've had an overflow in here before. The pegs for it are still in place," he added.

Together we hung the hammock. It rocked gently in the ship's sway and took up most of the space that was left in the cabin.

"And here." He opened the door of the cupboard I'd seen. Inside was dark as midnight but I discerned the shadowy shapes of his red coat and satin breeches and above, on a shelf, a fancy hat with a feather and a book that might be a Bible. "This door can be kept closed," he said. "You may be safe in here when you need to undress and dress."

I stepped into the darkness and pulled the door shut. There was the faintest scent of flowers, this scent pleasant, unlike the awful stink that surrounded my night visitor. Was it coming from my father's clothes? I moved a little toward the back to see what room there was and my foot touched something soft and bulky. What? I retreated, opened the door, stepped into the cabin again and peered where I had been.

"There is something in here," I said and reached to the back to pull it out. It was a soft drift of silky cloth and when I shook it out I saw that it was a woman's petticoat made of the darkest blue silk. The flower scent, lovely and delicate, wafted toward me.

I tried to gather my senses. What was this doing in my father's cupboard? It didn't belong to my mother. She had never been on board the *Reprisal* and this petticoat was fancier than any I'd seen her wear.

I held it out and my father took it. He gave me no explanation other than to say, "It must have fallen unnoticed off the peg."

I found it hard to look in his eyes. Had some lady been here with him? Had she shared with him this small mean cabin? Had they shared that narrow, cramped bed? But what about that open cabin door?

"You can leave your bundle of extra clothes in my cupboard," he said. I tried not to glance at the petticoat he still held. It scared me and I wished we could tear it in pieces and throw it overboard. I would, if I ever saw it again.

"Cap'n," a voice called through the open doorway.

I noticed how quickly my father put the rolled-up petticoat behind his back.

"All's safely stowed," the man said. "Cook says we be ready to eat." It was Herc, the man I was beginning to think of as our enemy. His smell choked the cabin.

"Thank ye, Herc." We waited till the fellow had gone, then I whispered, "Father? I have to tell you. That man was in our house. He was looking for something, and..."

"He was?" My father's voice hardened. "You are certain?"

I nodded, "That smell..."

"Did he see you?"

"Not clearly. I think he was looking for something."

I waited for him to offer an explanation. It was tempting to reveal that I'd once eavesdropped and knew there was something "they" wanted. But to tell that would be to admit to my shameful listening and I simply stood, silent.

"I am sorry that he frightened you," my father said at last. "There is something of value in our house. Several of my men suspect it's there. And it should not surprise me that one of them went so far as to search our house. I wish to say no more about it, Catherine. Such knowledge would only put you in danger. When the time comes, you will know all. I should tell you that I made you out to be younger because your voice does not have the timbre of a fifteen-year-old boy. Twelve years they will accept. But I will warn you again, Catherine. Charlie. A female on a ship can only be disaster."

I had a quick thought of the petticoat woman who had perhaps shared my father's cabin. Did my father still see her? And what of all those months when my mother had been sick and missing him? Had the secret woman been keeping him company then, taking my mother's rightful place?

"It's best we go now and eat," my father said, ending any further talk. "Afterward I will have you read and sign the Code of Conduct."

"Thank ye, Cap'n," I said, practicing my pirate language.

He stood in front of me and I remembered that he still held the blue silk petticoat behind his back. I moved past him through the open door but I turned my head and in the scratched, rusted mirror saw him raise the petticoat to his lips, then place it gently under the blanket on his bed.

For a second I wanted to cry.

He moved behind me.

"When you have signed the Code you will be a sworn member of the crew. There will be no turning back. Is that what you want, Charlie?" He touched my shoulder. "It is not too late. We will not weigh anchor till dawn. The rowboat can take you ashore tonight. I can get word to Bunty..." He stopped. "Do you want to stay or to go?"

I thought of all the misapprehensions I now had. I thought of my disillusionment with the ship, the dirt, the uncouth speech and manners of the men. I thought of Herc, the enemy, and the obvious animosity of his one-legged brother. But then I thought of the *Reprisal*, the way I'd seen her when she was floated at Cannon Cove. The shining, sleek shape of her. The way she seemed to lean forward, headed for adventure and ports unknown. I thought of the empty house that I used to call home, the house with no mother. My father was here. I loved him dearly and if he had transgressed, I still loved him.

"I will sign the Code," I said.

Chapter Six

My father left me on the deck, going across to where Mr. Trimble and some other men stood.

I wanted to wash my face and hands and I saw a bucket of water on the deck. The water was gray with scum on top. As I stood, disgusted, another pirate came by, plunged in his hands, gave them a rub and scoured them dry on a dirty piece of toweling.

"Fresh water's not easy to come by," he said as he passed me. "Cook has the use of it. You take what you can get, laddybuck."

This is all there is, I thought, and I closed my eyes and dipped my hands in above the wrists. But I couldn't bring myself to splash any of this on my face. I wiped my hands dry on the sides of my trousers.

Men were crowded around a wooden table with a steaming pot on it.

I crowded behind them.

The cook ladled food into my wooden bowl. It looked like a stew.

"Turtle," he grunted and threw some biscuits into the bowl too. "The green part is the fat. It's the best." He poked at it with the knife he held.

"Oh. Thank ye." I felt my stomach heave.

"And these biscuits, they're called hardtack." It was the cabin boy who seemed to be his helper giving me this information. "If you're thinkin' them's raisins in them you'd be wrong. Them's weevils. Myself, I like to eat them in the dark so as I don't see what I'm chewin' on."

Weevils? Weren't they like maggots? Insects of some kind?

He was grinning at me, his teeth white and even in the tan of his face. "Tap them on the side of your bowl afore ye eat. Sometimes them weevils will just pop out."

"Over here, young Charlie," someone called and I saw Red waving to me. He was sitting at a rough wooden table and he made space on the bench beside him. "Good grub today." He smacked his lips. "We caught us four fat turtles in the trees back there. Two for now and two still living for later. You turn them over on their backs and slit them down the middle. Don't be expecting vittles like this every day. With us it's feast or famine. Many's a time there's nothin'."

I could scarcely hear him because of the noise. The loud voices, the laughter, the belches, the clatter and clank of wooden bowls on the wooden table. And the smells! The smells of pirate sweat, mixed with cooked turtle and other odors I preferred not to think about. Would I ever get used to the smells of the *Reprisal?* Spilled rum sloshed over the table, lying in brown pools and running in little rivulets between the bowls.

I squeezed in the space beside Red.

He nudged me with an elbow. "Eat up. 'Twill put hair on your chest, like mine." He was still naked to the waist and he touched his red chest hairs with his greasy spoon.

I moved the food round on my plate but couldn't bring myself to put any to my mouth. Those raisin biscuits!

"Not hungry?" Red asked. "Nervous, I expect. You'll be swearing to the Code after. It's serious business. I mind when I took the oath for the first time I was a jabberin' fool. I had no notion what I signed. You'll be right though. I'll lay to that."

He eyed my plate. "I'll relieve you of that if you have

no mind to eat it."

In a second he'd changed plates with me and I had his empty one in front of me.

I saw my father, standing with Mr. Trimble and another man. They were eating heartily and swigging down jars of rum.

"That be the carpenter with your father and the quartermaster," Red said. "We got no surgeon on board so he does what's necessary. 'Twas him sawed off Hopper's leg and fitted him for the wooden one. Did a fine job of it, too."

"Hopper's the accordion man?" I asked.

"Aye. The very one." Red drained his jar of rum and gave a belch in which I could detect the mixed odors of liquor and meat. I tried not to breathe it in.

My father came striding toward us. "Ready, boy?" He eyed my empty plate. "You ate well. Come ye over here. It's a tradition to set on one of the cannons while ye hear the Code, and take the oath."

I nodded and followed him over to one of the four cannons on this side of the *Reprisal*. On his bidding, I slid up on it. In a few minutes, before he even unrolled the paper he carried, there were a dozen men around us. They were a raggedy-looking lot. Scurvy rats, I thought. Where were the kind of swashbuckling, romantic pirates

I'd imagined? My examples had been my father and Mr. Trimble and I could see now they weren't the pattern, especially when they were off the ship. The pirate standing next to me was picking his teeth with a splinter of wood and with his other hand scratching himself in a place not mentionable.

Where was Herc?

He was standing back, leaning against a coil of rope. His eyes glittered, black as coals. Was he thinking that if it weren't for me he could have had "it" in his possession by now?

My father unfolded the papers he held and began reading. I learned that each man should have a vote on all-important matters. That no man should gamble at dice or cards on board the ship. That all candles must be extinguished at eight at night.

The goats had wandered by to inspect the proceedings and now and then gave a bleat as if in agreement.

No pirate was to strike another aboard ship. I eased myself onto the hard cannon. The coldness of it moved through the bones of my back.

Now my father was reading about the musicians and I brought myself back to attention. We were allowed to rest on the Sabbath day, but for every other day we had to be available when asked. Just what Hopper had already told me. The captain and the quartermaster were to get the biggest share of the plunder taken and the rest was to be divided equally.

In a lower voice my father pronounced that the punishments for breaking the Code were severe: flogging, leg irons, or keelhauling. I didn't understand what the last two punishments meant, but they sounded unbearable. I was suddenly tense. Being a female aboard had not been listed, but I knew the punishment for that, and for aiding and abetting the presence of one, would be the same. I hoped I'd never find out firsthand what exactly leg irons and keelhauling were. Flogging I could imagine. The unwanted thought came. What of the blue petticoat lady? I wouldn't dwell on that.

Now and then I glanced up at Herc. I almost thought I could smell him from this distance.

By the time my father, the Cap'n, had finished reading the Code the crowd around us had grown bigger. I noticed how quiet they'd been during the ceremony, if that was what it was. To them, this was a solemn occasion. But after I'd signed "Charlie deVault" at the bottom of the paper my father gave me, the one that swore me to keep the oath, there was a smatter of cheering and yelling. More grog was passed and a wooden tankard of it was offered to me. I took it, swallowed a small sip and tried not to show my disgust at the taste.

"Well done, laddie boy!"

"You be a swab now, like the rest of us!"

"By damn we'll be glad to serve with you. By damn we will."

"Maaaa," said one of the goats and I saw the cabin boy rub the little nubby horns on its head and stroke the small gray beard that hung from its chin.

"It's gettin' late, lad," my father said to me. "And you need to be up afore sunrise. I'm wanted in the fo'c's'le. Get yourself some sleep. There's a lantern if you need it."

"I want to stay here on deck for a while," I said. "I have some pondering to do. It has been a strange day."

"Aye." His hand touched my shoulder and I saw the understanding and affection in his eyes. I also saw how quickly he hid his emotions. Another time in another place he would have wrapped his arms around me.

"Goodnight then."

I nodded. "Goodnight."

The men were drifting away. Herc had disappeared. Hopper still stood, glaring at me, scowling a black scowl. Suddenly he spewed a glob of spittle that landed on my foot. On my bare toes.

I stared down at it where it shimmied, brown and phlegmy.

My heart was beating too fast.

Some of the slime wobbled off as I walked toward him. "Why did you spit on me?"

"I meant for it to go over the side, laddie." His grin showed blackened teeth. I thought maybe the devil had a grin like that. Any pity I'd had for him had vanished. I knew the spittle had hit exactly where he'd wanted it to.

"Your aim's not good then," I said and I lifted my foot and wiped the glob off on the bottom of his trousers. "I'm giving back what's rightly yours."

"What..." he began. I sensed the fury in him and I saw the crutch move slightly. I stepped to the side.

He turned and with one last vile look stumped off along the deck.

My breathing was so loud and agitated I had to put a hand to my throat. But I was glad I had answered Hopper as I had. I had sworn to the oath, I was a pirate on board this ship and I had to be ready to take care of myself.

Chapter Seven

I was alone now except for the goats. I moved to the ship's railing.

The sun was setting, the sky pink and shot with gold over Cannon Bay. My heart quieted. The great dip in the sand where the *Reprisal* had been careened was filled now with seawater. The incoming and outgoing tide had washed away all traces of pirate feet. If the cliff behind the bay had not been there I could almost have seen the town and maybe even our house, up on Chancellor Hill, and the old graveyard where my mother was buried. Homesickness and loneliness and doubt rose up in me. Would I be able to live this life? And Hopper? I'd have to be with him, playing music with him, that horrible old man. My father had said I could still leave. But could I now, after I'd taken the oath? And if I left, would I regret it? It troubled me to think I would give up so easily.

The cabin boy, whose name I didn't know, was all at once beside me at the rail. "Pay no mind to Hopper. He's a grisly one all right."

"But what has he got against me?" I asked.

The cabin boy shrugged. "I won't tell you he'll get better with ye, for he won't."

"How encouraging," I muttered.

We were silent for a few minutes. "Hopper, he lost his leg to a cutlass, but that was before I joined the crew," the cabin boy said. " 'Fore it was taken off they made him roarin' drunk, but still I hear, when it was being sawed he howled like a sea wolf." I felt him glance sideways at me but I kept looking ahead. "Enough I expects to sour any man."

"I expect," I said. "But there's more."

"Aye, there's more." By the way he said the words I knew he was not going to enlighten me further.

A seagull swooped low, almost touching the mainmast, then skimmed off across the bay.

"I reckon he changed his mind about joining our ship," the boy said.

"How long have you been cabin boy?" I asked.

"A year, 'ceptin' for a month or two."

"What made you do it?"

"I wasn't meanin' to, and you can lay to that. I was walking down by the docks when I was picked up by two men twice my size and locked away." One of the goats came and rubbed against him. I almost thought I could hear it purr.

"You've heard of Davy Jones's Locker?" the boy asked. He stroked the goat's head. "There, Pansy," he whispered, "there."

"I know that it's another name for the bottom of the ocean where drowned sailors go," I said.

"Aye. But I'm here to tell you another meaning. There's a scoundrel by the name of Davy Jones who lives down on the docks. He has a cellar, dank and miserable it is, too. He picks up likely-looking and unsuspecting lads like myself and holds them there till he gets an offer from a pirate captain in need of a crew. Then he sells them."

I gasped. "You mean my father bought you?" Now I was facing him. The last of the sun edged his yellow hair making a halo of it, like a saint. But the rest of him wasn't saintly looking.

"He bought me. I begged him to. I'd had enough of Davy Jones's Locker. I thought I'd leave the *Reprisal* at some likely port and—" he stopped. Whatever he'd planned to do in some likely port was left unsaid. "But your father's a good captain and a fair one. I like the life on the *Reprisal*. It's free and betimes it's exciting. I've got me some gold now. I could still go ashore when a cruise is done and make a new life for myself. But I'm in no hurry now. There'll be more gold. When we capture a couple more ships, it'll be time enough for me to leave."

The goat had wandered off toward the galley where I supposed there might be some supper left for it.

We stood by the railing, not talking now. The sun had almost disappeared. It was the time of night that my mother called "the gloaming." I closed my eyes and the image of her came so clearly that I felt tears begin to squeeze from my eyes.

A roar came from the galley. "Get over here, you swab. There's work to be done."

"Cook," the boy said. "I was thinkin' he'd be soon after me. One of my jobs is to help him with the food and the cleaning up."

He turned to go, then spoke over his shoulder. "My name's William, if you were wondering."

William! I was glad to know his name, but I was wondering about something else. The way he'd talked to me. Was that how a boy spoke to another boy? I didn't think so. It was more like a young man talking to a young lady, telling her about himself. I was almost sure of it.

The gloaming was passing by now and dark was setting in. Around me men were laying out sleeping blankets on the deck, hanging hammocks, shouting among themselves. I'd already noticed how the pirates seldom talked quietly. Candles flickered. Hadn't there been something in the Code about putting out candles after eight of a night? I had to go now, retrace my earlier route and find my father's cabin.

The lantern had already been lit. I suspected my father had come down ahead of me and done that so I could see my way. My hammock swung gently on its hooks. It was all so strange, the small cabin filled with yellow light so unlike any place I'd ever slept before. As for the hammock, I eyed it warily. Could I really sleep in that?

I glanced at my father's narrow bed. There was no bump under the blanket. He'd taken away the petticoat, the one that had belonged to someone dear to him. I blinked away an unexpected tear. The door to the long cupboard was closed. I opened it, saw my parcel of clothes and untied the string. There were changes of clothes and I decided that, even if couldn't wash myself, I could put on something clean. I found a shirt, tighter than the one I was wearing now, the one that could ease itself up and reveal me. This would be better.

I set my flute up on the shelf and had just stepped out of my canvas trousers when I heard someone coming. The cabin door was open, as my father had said it was all the time. I quickly pulled the door of the cupboard closed and was immediately in darkness, except for a slit of lantern light that came through a crack at the side. Whoever was in the cabin was moving quietly. Was it my father, come down after all?

I peered through the slit. The man's back was toward me but I recognized him for who he was. Herc, the big ox-like man who had climbed the rope into the *Reprisal* carrying Hopper on his back! There was no mistaking the bulk of him, the square-shaped head, the earring that gleamed gold in the lantern light. Should I wriggle into my trousers, open the door and ask, "Are you looking for my father?" Or should I stay hidden and wait for him to leave? I was watching him, one eye pressed to the slit.

What was he doing? There was an air of secrecy about the way he moved, so quietly, so furtively, looking under the blanket on my father's bed, putting it squarely back in place, kneeling to pull out the sea chest under the wooden dresser. I saw him try to lift the lid but my father must have kept it locked because it didn't open.

He passed the desk, ignoring the papers that were

spread on it, then came toward the cupboard. His big shoulder brushed the hammock and set it to swaying, the shadows jumping wildly off the walls. There was danger here. I sensed it. I could smell it. I moved as quietly as I could to the back of the cupboard, to the darker recesses where I had found the petticoat earlier today.

He opened the door. His bulk blocked the opening and then he stepped inside. The floor creaked under his weight. He reached up to the shelf and pushed my flute to the side. He took down the hat with the feather and ran his hands around the brim, as if searching, put it back, felt down the legs of the trousers my father had worn, felt along the sleeves of the shirt.

He peered into the dark darkness where I stood. My heart hammered so loudly I was afraid he would hear. Goosebumps prickled along my bare legs. I moved slightly and the floorboard gave a creak that seemed to me as loud as a firecracker. Surely he had heard.

But someone else was coming. I prayed that it would be my father, though I knew already that it wasn't. I knew who it was. Thump-tap, thump-tap, thump-tap. It was Hopper, his wooden leg and his crutch betraying his approach.

Herc stepped back into the cabin and closed the cupboard door. I was in darkness again and so afraid of alerting them to my presence that I didn't dare move to see again through the slit.

They were talking, whispering, and I strained to hear but no words came to me.

I heard them leave. But then there was a chuckle, so full of malevolence that my blood chilled and words, loud enough for me to hear. Herc's voice.

"Be he dead or alive."

I heard them leave.

There was only silence.

It was a long while after that before I came out of the cupboard.

Chapter Eight

I didn't climb into the hammock. Instead I sat in the chair by the desk, trembling inside, wondering what I'd seen and heard. It was a relief when my father came.

He sensed that I was disturbed. "Catherine?" he asked. "What is it? Tell me!" When he spoke my true name like that I felt better.

I wet my lips. "I was changing. I was in the cupboard," I said, and I told him about Herc and Hopper searching the cabin and the words I'd heard.

"I felt sure they'd find me," I said. "Those words, 'Be he dead or alive.' I think they meant you. I don't think they meant me."

My father bent and kissed the top of my head. No one to see: no one to remark on this strange behavior with a son who was a new pirate.

"Are they searching for a map to buried treasure? With an X-marks-the-spot?" I asked. "I've read of treasure maps. . . ."

He smiled. "No treasure map. I've never seen one. I believe they are only in stories. I've been amused by many a forged one, sold to some fool on the docks. But if any of my crew has gold to spare he'll spend it in port, on rum and on the ladies, and you can lay to that."

I reached for his hand. Sometimes, when he was home from the sea and he sat in his big leather chair with me on his lap, reading to me, telling me tales of the sea, but never of pirates, he held my hand like this. I knew the rough feel of his hand, the little bump in the middle of the palm. I rubbed it now the way I always did.

"They don't bury treasure," he went on and it was his storytelling voice, lulling me, reassuring me. "And they do not leave maps for others to find and dig up what they've hidden."

"Mr. Hopper doesn't take to me," I said, bringing him back to the present. "I need to watch how I go when he's around."

"You give yourself good advice," my father said.

I wasn't going to tell him about the gob of spit. Pirates didn't whine, or complain to the captain about their shipmates. Pirates are not chicken-hearted.

"He doesn't take to you because of me," my father said. "He bargained hard with the men to have his brother made cap'n on the last vote. He did not succeed. Now he has you to torment. I must tell you honestly that I do not know what to do about this. I blame myself for bringing you and putting you in such danger."

"It was I who persuaded…" I began, but my father held up his hand.

"I ought not to have been persuaded." He sighed. "How will I ever explain it to your mother when we meet again?"

He meant in heaven. They would never meet again till then.

I looked up at his face. His eyes were closed and I saw that his lips trembled at the thought of my mother.

"She will understand," I whispered.

"But now you are here," he went on. "And there is no way out till the voyage is over. I will try my best to protect you from them. I must draw no special attention to you though. Can you tolerate it, Catherine?"

"I can," I said and I hoped I would be able to keep my word on that.

"Off with you to your hammock then," my father said and he helped me slide in. Getting in was not easy. He gave me the blanket from his bed.

"Tomorrow I'll set William to find another one for me."

I lay in the hammock listening to his breathing. It took it a long time for it to change into the deep breath of sleep.

I was glad of his presence.

I'd told my father of the two men in his cabin. I had told him I could tolerate their scheming and stay away from them. Now I should put them out of my mind. But the remembrance of their stealth and the cunning slant of their words pushed sleep away from me.

I pulled the blanket tight around me.

I'd think about the cabin boy, William. My mother and I had lived such a sheltered life that I had been in contact with few boys or young men. I had been acquainted with some. Mr. Travers, who came each day to give me lessons, had a son called Henry who was my age. We sometimes, with my mother's permission, studied together. But I did not think of him when he wasn't there. He did not fill my mind as I was discovering William did. Then there'd been Eli who sometimes delivered our groceries. He had tried to kiss my cheek once but I had pushed him away. I had no interest in him, and I could barely remember him now, but William! Perhaps it was his yellow hair that so attracted me. Or the look of him, shirtless, coiling a rope or scrubbing the deck. Or that scar, like a white thread across his face. Sometime, maybe, I would ask him how he came by it.

I turned abruptly in my hammock so that it swayed in an arc so wide I was fortunate not to fall on the floor like a fish tumbling out of a net.

It was only then that I realized that my father had not told me what Herc and Hopper were searching for, or where it was hidden. He had indicated that I would be safer the less I knew.

When my thoughts and the hammock settled I tried again for sleep. Its gentle sway now brought the faint remembrance of a cradle, and my mother rocking me and singing to me about a beautiful lake in Scotland, and a lost love, gone forever. I thought of my mother lying now at peace on Cob Hill. Sadness swept over me and tears ran down my face. But in spite of that, I slept.

"Up, up, up, young laddie." It was Red, shaking the hammock, sprawling me out on to the floor. "They be needing music," he said. "We're setting sail, me boy, and they likes a good song to go along wi' it."

Hopper was already on deck. "You lazy pup," he snarled at me. "Are you to be wakened like a child at every sunup?"

I gave him stare for stare.

Red tucked his fiddle under his chin and winked at me. "Well, laddiebuck, we're off on our journey."

The *Reprisal* was underway, dipping her bowsprit into the blue of the ocean, spray rising on either side like two misted ghosts. There were shouts of, "Keep her near to the wind," and "Pull her up, you shirking lubbers."

We played on our instruments for hours. My lips were sore from the mouthpiece and my head started to thump, complaining of the music. The decks were alive with barefoot, sweaty men, rushing back and forth. Words were shouted, some in a language I didn't understand and there was singing, to tunes I didn't know but that I quickly learned.

Red's foot tapped ceaselessly and Hopper's sour face never changed—whatever we were playing.

"Fifteen men on a dead man's chest

Yo ho ho and a bottle of rum."

Red nodded toward a man rolling an oversized chest along the deck. "Rum," he said, "a hogshead full. There'll be plenty of it drunk the night."

I was surprised when the men joined in with gusto

when Hopper struck up a mournful tune.

"To the mast nail our flag it is dark as the grave,

Or the death which it bears while it sweeps o'er the wave."

Then one of the crew, a tall, thin man with tattoos on his legs and arms shouted, "The gibbet'll be the end for most of us, so time enough to be singin' of death when we're hangin' there. Give us another shanty, mates, a cheery one this time."

Red nodded and started on a hearty hornpipe. But I kept thinking of the words of the death song. Hanging would be the final punishment for a captured pirate. Probably hanging in a metal cage in a town square, for all to see. And I was a pirate. My father too, and fat Red, and Mr. Trimble who liked my mother's lingonberry wine, and blue-eyed William.

We'd have to be caught first.

After a while Hopper set his accordion down on the deck, nodded toward the stern and grunted, "I'll be back."

"It's his time of day for the seats of easement," Red said. "Goes like clockwork, he does. An' we get a break."

"Why is he the boss, anyway?" I asked.

"His brother," Red said with no more explanation.

He and I stood waiting by the railing.

The *Reprisal* slapped briskly through the ocean. Three

dolphins swam alongside.

"Mermaids they be," Red pronounced. "Sea changelings. When they feel the mood they'll make themselves other than what ye see. Beautiful girls they'll be, with seaweed twined in their long fair hair, and scales that shimmer like emeralds. Oh aye, I seen them a few times and tried to catch me one, but they keep themselves out of reach."

The sea sizzled past us, the sky moved, and the dolphin dipped and rose and gamboled alongside. The mast of the *Reprisal* cut across the clouds like a great finger, pointing, pointing. The lookout stood high in the crow's nest, keeping watch through his spyglass, sweeping the empty sea for an enemy ship or for a likely vessel for us to attack. I wondered how he could endure it up there, the ship swaying and tossing beneath him.

"Hey, you lazy seadogs. Over here. There's men working and would like some music." Hopper's voice cut through our silence.

"He's finished," Red said to me and we went back to our music.

We followed the same routine day after day. Many days passed. There was no sign of an enemy chasing us or a vessel to capture and plunder.

The men worked at their shipboard duties and we played the accompaniment. I was getting to know them even though they paid me no mind. I knew most of the names and which of them to stay away from when I could. Herc and Hopper McDonald were high on that list.

I learned that someone had to be always at the bilge pumps. And that there were rats aplenty down in those bilges, rats as big as a man's leg.

"We had a ship's cat," Red told me, "but he ran off on Cannon Beach. He was scared of them rats. Some were bigger'n he was."

The thought of rats made me shiver.

There were sails to be mended. There were musket balls to be made, the molten lead poured into molds. There were decks to be scrubbed, guns to be cleaned.

I saw William mostly at a distance. But one day he came over to me with a stick of dried beef. "I stole this out of cook's store for you. A growin' lad needs strengthenin' grub and I notice you don't eat more'n a sparrow."

The beef was hard and tough as leather but I held on to the knowledge that he had noticed me, growin' lad though he thought I was, and I thought on his words for days.

I made friends with one of the goats. Her name was Daisy and she took to following me around and lying close when we played our music.

Hopper was always shooing her away. One day he lunged out at her with his crutch.

I grabbed the end of it before he could jab her. "Leave her alone," I said. "She's doing no harm."

"She's under me foot. I'll knock her senseless if she don't keep her distance," Hopper snarled. "She'll be leavin' us soon, anyways. Cook'll be cuttin' her throat and servin' her up in a good salmagundi." He licked his lips. "Tasty fare, goat. Ye'll love it, laddie."

I knelt and hugged Daisy and kissed her ears and told her not to listen to him. But I knew what he said was true and I could hardly bear it.

There were times when there was nothing else for the men to do but play cards and roll dice. They didn't gamble. The Code forbade it but they kept score and "when we has gold we'll be payin' our debts." They told and retold stories of prizes taken and cap'ns they'd sailed with. There were fistfights, and I thought it a wise thing that the Code forbade knife fights aboard. They shot their muskets over the railings and there was always the stink of gunpowder to mix with the other smells on deck. They tattooed one another. I'd stop and watch when they weren't demanding a tune. But they liked music and wanted it on every occasion.

"Look 'ere, lad," Fish, who was doing the tattooing, shouted at me. "Will I paint a pretty picture on you?"

I shook my head and stepped back but curiosity brought me forward to see. To see the skin on an arm or a back or a chest scratched till it bled and gunpowder poked into the bleeding slit.

"By my oath, that's a fine 'un. A Skull and Crossbones, good as the flag we flies under."

"Not often enough, me hearty. Not often enough."

It was true. We hadn't spotted a vessel since we left port six days ago.

The crew was on edge with waiting. They grumbled and swore.

"Hey, lookout. Are ye asleep up there? Call us a sail!"

And it was the next day they got what they wanted.

"A sail! A sail!" the lookout shouted and pointed to starboard, leaning so far out of the crow's nest it was by God's grace that he didn't fall.

And the men were suddenly alive again, scrambling to their feet, scattering cards and dice, squeezing the railing. My father came to be among them. He and Mr. Trimble had their spyglasses. I saw William, close to the front. And I saw the ship, in the distance, coming like a phantom out of the mist, phantom sails ballooning.

My father shouted an order and the *Reprisal*'s bow

veered a little to starboard.

I could tell that now we were on a new course. One that would take us close by her.

I was about to be in my first sea battle.

Chapter Nine

*T*he distance between the two ships grew less.

Red saw me glancing up at our flag.

"French flag," he said. "Very friendly-like." His little teeth showed, white pearls shining through his red beard. "Once we gets closer..." He ran a finger across his throat. "That be when the Jolly Roger shows hisself and the excitement begins."

It was easy to see he was overjoyed. He was a pirate. This was his life. I was a pirate too. I seemed to have to keep telling myself that. But pirate was only a word. I hadn't had to act like a pirate yet nor had I seen pirates in action. Soon that would change. My stomach felt full of weevils.

Red squinted against the sun. "She be a small frigate. She'll be carryin' no more'n sixty men. I count eight guns. There'll be another eight to port."

Now we were close enough to see her flag.

"English," Red observed.

I read the name in gold across her stern. *Golden Bird*.

Something brushed against my leg. I looked down and saw Daisy.

"No, no," I said and I circled her neck with my arm and urged her in behind the doors to the deck.

There was a sudden whoop from the crew of the *Reprisal* and a lubbing clatter as our French flag came down and the Skull and Crossbones went up in its place.

"Fooled 'em," Red hollered.

I saw the crew of the *Golden Bird* scrambling across her deck.

On the *Reprisal* men manned the cannons, three to a gun. And there was William, feeding an iron cannonball into one of the wide muzzles. The gunner, a man named Quicken, stood ready to fire. Along the deck the other guns were prepared, ready for duty.

There was a jabber of talk on the deck and then the swish of a rope being thrown. I heard the thump as the grappling hook on the end of it landed on the deck of the other ship. It didn't catch the first time and we all watched and catcalled as it was thrown again. This time it took hold.

We were connected.

That was when my father's voice boomed, loud and commanding.

"On board the *Golden Bird*. Surrender, or we'll sink ye!"

A cannon shot from the *Reprisal* blasted across her bow.

"We have no likin' to sink her," Red whispered to me. "We want what's on her, and we don't want it to plunge into Davy Jones's Locker. Disablin' her, that'll be the plan. We'll board her and pick her clean."

"But they'll fight," I said. "They'll not let us just take their cargo and go."

"Oh aye, they might fight. But they could give up before we get started. Many's a one does that. It's the sight of the flag and the sight of our guns and the look of our crew when we start wavering, us being cutthroats 'n all."

"You two! Are yez havin' a good conversation?" Hopper yelled.

"Music, ye vermin, music."

We began playing and I couldn't believe what I was seeing.

The crew was going crazy. They thumped and jumped and waved their arms at the *Golden Bird*. They ran in circles, brandishing their muskets and axes and cutlasses. Their screams were like people in agony, like Banshees, like an animal caught in a trap, like a man being burned at the stake.

"What are they doing?" I had to shout make myself heard.

"That's wavering," Red shouted back. "It's to scare the britches off the enemy."

They were savages in some far off jungle, dancing around the cooking pot.

Bile rose in my throat.

And our "music" was not music at all. Just sounds. Horrible sounds.

"Make noise, more noise," Hopper screamed.

Hopper and Red could yell as they played. And our instruments shouted and screeched out discordant notes and chords. The accordion was a pig squealing, the fiddle and the flute were cats shrieking, witches screeching. It was music from Hell.

"Lookee there!" Hopper shouted proudly and there was Herc, a cutlass in each hand, twirling them so the sun flashed across them like fire, throwing them in the air, catching them, throwing them again, all the time dancing some devilish dance.

Sweat ran down from my armpits, trickled over my stomach and made blotches on my clothing.

I stopped for another second and Hopper poked me with a bony elbow.

"Scare 'em, boy! Scare the lights out o' them!"

Once I caught Red's eye and he winked. He was relishing this.

"Are ye ready to surrender?" My father's voice again.

His answer came right away with a fusillade of shots from the other ship.

"That's good," Red shouted. "They got somethin' to protect. Fine plunder for us."

One of our men, I knew his name, Clegg, jumped for the rope between the ships and swarmed across it. I only heard one shot. It missed Clegg but there was a splash as he lost his balance and fell into the sea.

"Help!" I called, running to the railing, but Hopper's voice stopped me. "Get back here, ye sick whelp. Let him be. He'll be back on the ship or he'll be drowned. 'Tis nothin' to you."

A cannon blasted from our deck and one of the *Bird*'s masts crashed into pieces.

"Surrender, ye dogs," my father called. "Ye're finished."

But they did not surrender.

Our men slithered across, swinging on ropes and dropping on the *Golden Bird*'s deck.

We had been pulled closer so there was such a narrow space between us and them that some of the men jumped. Some made it. Some fell in the sea. Our bowsprit jutted out almost touching the *Golden Bird*'s deck and our men squirmed across it, hand over hand.

We played our music, alone on the *Reprisal*'s deck except for the gunners and their helpers. The guns on both ships blasted away. I glanced often at William who kept feeding his cannon. And I was glad he was here and not part of the fighting on board the *Golden Bird*.

She listed to port where a shell had struck her and from where we stood we could clearly see down onto her deck. My father was on that deck, fighting with his men. I saw him once, clashing hand to hand with another man. Father, oh father, I begged, but not aloud. I pray to God you will be safe. Can this be you, so fierce, so bloodthirsty? You, my beloved father?

At some point I became numb. Nothing was real. Not the blood that ran bright along the deck, not the slashing and the savagery. I knew I was seeing things I would never forget that would forever come back to me in dreams. I tried not to look and then I realized that I could close my eyes and keep playing. I could still hear the shouts,

THE PIRATE CAPTAIN'S DAUGHTER

the screams of the wounded, the curses and the threats. I played my loudest to block my ears and found I was playing the same note over and over and over and over, and that my ears rang and ached and that the stinging on my face came from secret tears.

It ended at last. *The Golden Bird* had two great holes blasted in her side. Emptied of the riches she'd been carrying, her crew beaten and finished she skulked away. But not until all of her gold and the diamonds she had been carrying and had fought so hard for were transferred to the *Reprisal*.

Our crew, bedraggled, exhausted, wounded but not broken, victorious and rejoicing, huddled on the deck.

There were shouts of "That's a bird as won't be flyin' for a while," and "A bit less golden than when she met up with us. She'll think twice afore she takes on a crew like our 'uns again."

Rum splashed into wooden cups. Wounds were examined and pronounced "Nothin' much" even when they were gashed from shoulder to groin. The ship's carpenter was called upon to do what needed to be done with his sail needle and twine but he was brushed off. "No need of you, mate. We got better things to do."

The ship was examined and pronounced hurt and hammered but strong enough for a dozen more voyages.

"We can caulk her boards and mend her shrouds and we'll be needin' to sail with one side higher to keep the water from floodin' in where some of the bullets got us. But she'll be right and tight and no harm done."

I looked for Clegg and saw him lying at ease, swigging down rum. I didn't know which of the others had fallen into the sea and nobody spoke of them, drowned or safe.

My father spilled the diamonds and piled the gold pieces of eight on the deck. There was a roar of delight.

Eyes gleamed. Backs were clapped and there was a babble of exultation.

"I knowed the plunder would be plenty by the way they fought to save it," Red announced.

"Aye and ye were right."

My father divided the takings according to the Code. Two shares to the captain and quartermaster, one and a half to the gunners, and the rest divided according to importance. William picked his allotment up and tied it in a red handkerchief. Some had pouches that they tied around their necks. Some held their booty tight in their fists.

The musicians were included in the dividing.

My father's eyes did not meet mine as he put my share in front of me.

"Will I keep it safe for ye, Charlie?" he asked and I

nodded. I didn't want the blood money. But that could be attended to later.

"Ye did well, young un," somebody called. "I'd say ye're a good addition to the crew."

"Thank ye," I muttered.

There was some squabbling over which diamonds were bigger and which smaller and if everything was fair. One that was a good size was smashed with the carpenter's hammer and the pieces divvied up. When all appeared satisfied Herc called out: "Musicians! Give us the victory tune." His sickening smell wafted in my direction.

I wrinkled my nose.

"He has a bad smell about him day and night," Red whispered to me. " 'Tis an affliction. So he doses it with perfume he took off of a Frenchie. I calls it 'Perfum de Corpse' But not to his face and you can lay to that." He gave me another of his wicked winks.

"Music, I said," Hopper yelled again and at his nod we struck up and the men sang with so much lustiness and energy it was as if they had not faced the knife or the cutlass or death in the past hours.

"I fight, 'tis for vengeance! I love to see flow,
At the stroke of my saber, the life of my foe,
I strike for the memory of long-vanished years.
I only shed blood where another sheds tears."

It was a song so horrible, verse after verse, that I had to sniff and choke to keep my tears from flowing again.

I looked at William.

His face was blackened with gunpowder. The scar on his face gleamed in the last of the light. How had he felt about today? I thought it might have been a ball from his cannon that had first disabled the *Golden Bird*, but it had been Quicken, not William who'd fired the first shot and the ones that came after. I noticed that William did not join in the shouts of the singers and I wasn't sure what that meant.

Perhaps it meant he hated this the way I did.

Or perhaps it only meant that he didn't know the words.

Chapter Ten

There was carousing on the deck, drunken carousing till almost daybreak while the men danced and sang and the musicians played. I had never been so exhausted. I relived the battle with the *Golden Bird*. Where was she now? Had she sunk and were all her remaining crew down in Davy Jones's Locker with the bones of the seamen who'd gone there before them?

My father left me alone. He had warned me there would be no special treatment from him and he'd kept his word. I was there with the rest of his crew while he stayed with Mr. Trimble and the sail master.

Hopper played his accordion, one handed, stomping

away with his wooden leg and Red stopped time after time "To wet his whistle," he said.

"To drown it more like," Fish yelled.

William came across to me. "Ye had yer baptism, Charlie. What do ye think? Do you still want to be a pirate?"

"I'm pondering it," I said.

Somebody had caught two bilge rats and was trying to make them drink rum through a pipe. There were roars of laughter till one of the rats bit Herc's finger and he grabbed a rat tail in each hand, swung the poor creatures to the counting of the crew and tossed them overboard. Then there was much speculation about how soon it would take them to drown and which one would drown first.

I thought the night would never end.

When at last the musicians were freed and I slithered into my hammock I expected to sleep immediately. But I was still awake when my father came to his cabin. He shaded the lantern light with his hand and I saw him go to his sea chest and unlock it. He took out the silk petticoat and held it to his face.

Should I speak? Make my wakefulness known? But the moment seemed so private that I turned my head away and stayed quiet.

I heard him relock the box.

I must have made a small sound that told him I was

still awake.

"Catherine?" His voice was husky. "I have not told you about the petticoat you saw that first day. Perhaps this is the right time. I chose not to speak of it before, to cause you more unhappiness and give you more sadness."

I moved a little so I could see his face, though it was hard to distinguish his features in the shadows cast by the lantern.

"The petticoat I hold so dear was your mother's. I bought it for her in St. George on the day we were married. It was silly and flamboyant but she wore it all the time we were there. The perfume, too. I don't believe she ever wore either of them again."

He paused and I saw that now his eyes were closed, as if he were remembering.

Tears choked my throat. Poor Father!

"I carry it with me on all my journeys. It helps with the loneliness. Now, now that she is gone, I can hardly bear it. I loved her so."

We were both quiet, the swaying of the *Reprisal* strangely comforting.

Then he gave a little cough. "The men would not like it. They would deem it a sign of weakness, not befitting a pirate captain."

He bent and kissed my forehead and I thought the

air around him held still the faint smell of her wedding perfume.

"Goodnight, Catherine."

He turned and climbed into his bunk and I lay for a long time, listening to the sound of his breathing, knowing the minute that he finally slept.

It was still dark when I woke. I turned my head and saw my father's bunk was empty. No Red, pulling me awake. Were the men allowed to sleep late after a victory? It didn't seem likely.

I lay for a few moments, remembering my father's words of last night. I was here now, and though I could not reveal myself to be his daughter, I could share his loneliness.

I swung out onto the floor. No need to get dressed. That was how I slept. Sometimes I thought longingly of my soft flannel robes, even the ugly gray one that Aunt Louise had sent me. But being already right for the day the minute I wakened had its advantages. The floor seemed to be swaying more than usual. The door to the cupboard that I carefully kept closed had opened and now swung toward me and back. I had a moment of panic. Had someone come searching again while we slept? But that wasn't what was happening. Everything in the cabin that could slither was slithering. My father's hat with the feather was lying at my feet. It had tumbled off the cupboard shelf and made its way across the floor. My mother's brush and comb set was a jumbled pile on his dresser.

Were we sinking? Had we been damaged so badly that now we were going down? I needed to get up on deck. We couldn't be sinking. My father would never have left me here if there were danger.

I hurried as carefully as I could, stepping around the casks, old sails and ropes that were at a slant, too heavy to slide about.

I heard Red's fiddle, sawing out a halfhearted hornpipe. I was almost blinded by a flash of white light, followed by a rumble, then lightning, thunder, and a sea that chopped and slashed against the ship's hull.

The deck streamed with rain.

Men were at work, rain streaking down on their bare backs as they plugged up the shot holes in the *Reprisal*'s sides. The sails were down, but the lookout was still on the mainmast. How terrible to be up there in this weather! Red stood in the lee of a bulwark, sawing on his fiddle.

Clothes were strewn across the deck—trousers, shirts, weskits, underdrawers. The rain sliced down on them. It took me a few seconds to understand. This must be wash-the-clothes-day. Rain was doing their work for them. Not that they ever considered washing clothes anyway. The thought of having clean garments was so enticing that I decided to go back down to my father's cabin and bring up my few pieces of clothing. I had already washed them twice in seawater and they were stiff as planks and rubbed my skin. I'd bring my father's clothes, too, I decided.

First, I thought I should speak to Red and see if he had need of me. I'd tell him I'd be back with my flute.

I was about to make my way across to him when I looked down and saw that what I was wearing was already soaked. And I saw more. My loose shirt was pasted against my body and there, plain as day, were my bosoms as if on display.

I gasped and quickly covered my top with my arms. Had anyone seen me? And what about my lower half? I leaned forward to make sure but my canvas trousers had only turned black and not transparent. The men were all bent over, at work, and I turned fast, so my back was to them. There was a canvas shirt on a hook in the cupboard that was big and would cover me. I'd rush back down and get it.

"Charlie!" It was William, stumbling toward me, barefoot on the wet deck, sliding a half barrel in front of him. "Take the edge of this," he called. "We need to save some rain water. 'Tis scarce on board as fleas on eggs. Cap'n wants this 'un and another put over here, away from the repairs. It'll be lippin' laggin' with good fresh water in no time."

I stood where I was, my back to him, my arms still crossed across myself.

"Do ye not hear me? What's wrong, boy? Have ye hurt yerself?"

I couldn't get words out.

"Well, gi' me a hand here." He was impatient now, standing in the rain, his yellow hair plastered against his head, water running in little streams down his bare chest.

"Ye *are* hurt! Let me see."

He was sliding toward me.

"I'm not hurt. It's... that I have to go back to the cabin and..." I spoke over my shoulder and took a step, just as the *Reprisal* lurched and threw me against a coil of rope. I stretched out a hand to save myself, realized in that instant that William was beside me, saw me, really saw me.

His blue eyes widened. He stared.

I covered myself again with my arms but I knew it was too late. I turned myself away from him and pressed against the rough wetness of the rope.

Behind me, William's voice again. "Well, I'll just be

goin' then," and I heard the difference in the way he spoke. There was an embarrassment now. The man-to-man voice had disappeared.

The coil of rope stabbed at my skin. It smelled of tar and something like wet animal.

I risked a sideways glance at William.

He was standing motionless, looking out across the rise and fall of the gray ocean.

I almost couldn't hear him when he spoke.

"I'll not be telling," he said and then he was gone.

Chapter Eleven

I stood in the cabin, water dripping off my wet clothes onto the floor. What had just happened? William now knew I was a girl.

I was shivering and my teeth were chattering so hard my head shook. My father and I were in mortal danger. Everything depended on William. I remembered his last words. "I won't be telling." But could I trust him? He was a pirate with the same superstitions they all had.

I found the canvas shirt in the cupboard, stripped off my wet top and put it on. It was so big and so long it came down over my thighs. So much the better. There was a spurt of weak lightning and then a ripple of thunder, far away now across the sea. The storm was easing. Daisy and Pansy were quiet and the hens' clucking had a calmer sound.

I took my flute from the cupboard shelf and went back up on deck.

Where was William? The thought of him was a nervous tremor in my stomach and a sort of smothered excitement. I couldn't help it. My mind kept straying back to that moment when he saw me as a girl, the realization in his eyes, the shock and then... then what? Nothing. He'd turned away. I told myself not to go thinking like a girl in a trashy book, the kind I hid from my mother, a stupid girl who expected a love story. Still. I had to push the imaginings of a tender meeting from my mind. A scene where he said, "Now I know why I always had such strange feelings toward you. It is almost as if I knew all the time." We would be in some dark, secluded corner of the deck. I would reach up and run my finger along the thin white scar on his face. I'd ask him how he came by it and he'd lean over and kiss...

"Stop!" I might have said it out loud but there was no one to hear me. More likely he would ignore me. That was, if he didn't disclose what I was.

"I won't be telling," he'd said and I thought I believed him.

I was out on the deck now. The rain had ceased but the

sky was still bundled with dark clouds. The crew worked, caulking the pistol holes, mending the topsail, which had taken a shot from the *Golden Bird*.

The two half barrels were in place, each one quarter filled with rain water. But where was William?

The deck was slippery with rain over grease. I went carefully around the spread-out pirate clothes that were littered everywhere. Not mine or my father's. I had neglected to bring them up on the deck, being too consumed by my recent encounter with William.

"Is Hopper not playing today?" I asked Red.

Red scraped his bow across his fiddle strings to make a noise like a cat with a stepped-on tail. "Got a fire in his belly," he said. "Too much rotgut last night." He sighed. "Ah well, there's many a man is worse today. Tew has been busy, sewin' and cuttin' and sawin' and givin' out potions. I swear, what with the drink half the crew didn't feel their pains and their losses till this mornin'."

Tew was the carpenter and surgeon. I hadn't had occasion to see him yet myself but I knew he was the one who'd taken off Hopper's leg on a different journey.

Red and I were alone. He had been on the *Reprisal* a long time and knew many things. I made a decision.

"Red?" I said. "There is something my father has that Herc wants, something of great value. Can you tell me what it is?"

Red loosened and tightened the pegs on his violin. "Aye, I could tell you. I could tell you what happened. 'Tis maybe your right to know. Here's the way of it. The *Reprisal* captured another pirate ship name of The *Cormorant*. This was a while back. There was plunder and plenty of it to be divided. Happy as they were, the crew wanted to sew the cap'n's lips together and burn out one of his eyes, for jollity like, since he had killed a couple of our'n. He'd a' been butchered in the end and you can lay to that. Your father, the cap'n, had dealin's with the other cap'n afore, and he pleaded wi' the crew, and saved him in the end. The other cap'n, his name was Brigham, in gratitude for his life, gave your father a ruby, big as a navy bean and red as fire. He'd taken it himself off of a merchant ship bound for the Indies. It's called the Burmese Sunrise and it's a sight to see. Worth a prince's ransom.

"The men got wind of what was given and thought it should be divided, since that Cap'n Brigham was part of the plunder, and he maybe had hid it somewheres on the *Cormorant*. But your father stood firm. ''Twas a gift', he said, and exchanged on neutral ground. He near was voted out as cap'n there and then. But some of the men liked it that he was strong and stood up for hisself. There's them as still think he owes it to 'em, though. Meself, now,

I think 'tis rightfully his. An' that's the story."

"Thank you, Red," I said. "I'm taking a minute away, but I'll be back." I needed time to think about what he'd told me. About the mercy my father had shown, about his reward, about his strength.

I sloshed to the bow holding on to one of the railings to keep my balance. The ruby was what Herc and Hopper and maybe some of the others were searching for. Where was it? Herc had gone as far as to break into our house. Where could it be?

I stood for a few moments by the red dragon figurehead letting it prop me up. From here I could tell that the ship was sailing level again and that the sea that stretched in front of us as far as I could see still looked angry. No waves, just a nasty jumble of small gray and white tips that fought against each other and against the hull of the *Reprisal*. Spray lashed my face and when I licked my lips I tasted salt.

It was time to go back.

Red and I played, and the men sang as they worked. They sang of Cap'n Kidd and Joe Jelly who fought a shark and ate its belly, and a ship called the *Fancy* that beached on the rocks in Portuguese Bay. They were jolly enough tunes but their hearts did not seem to be in them. And I, playing, let my thoughts wander over our old home in Port Teresa, visualizing room to room. A ruby, big as a navy bean, and red as fire.

"It's hard to lose some of our crew," Red said, when we finished. "One shot through the chest, one slashed so bad Tew could do nothin' for him and one drowned when he fell as he was climbin' up the side o' the *Bird*." He shook his head. "An ear lost, too, and a hand that'll never pull up a riggin' no more. Last I saw, Tew was pickin' wood splinters out of Saracan's chest. Them wood splinters that fly off the deck be as sharp as daggers. Flyin' six-inch daggers and ye'll never dodge them, I'll lay to that."

I closed my eyes.

Red sighed, then grinned. "Still and all, the plunder was good. No complaints from any quarter."

"You'd think they'd have enough without..." I stopped and gave Red a sideways look.

"Aarg! There's never enough," Red said.

"Who was it was shot?" I asked.

"Paulie. Better for him than for Thomas. Took *him* a while to pass on. And drownin's quick and right for a seaman. But I 'spects Thomas had no wish to try it this early, him bein' just a young lad."

I swallowed hard. Paulie and Thomas and Saracen! I'd known all of them to see and Thomas had told me one day his father played the flute, too.

"Is it not usual to lose this many men?" I asked, hoping

to hear that it was normal. Surely I wasn't becoming superstitious as they were, wondering if it was because of their bad luck, having a woman aboard. I being the woman.

Red shrugged. "It happens. We don't like it. I 'spects that's why we drown our sorrows with demon rum."

I felt desolate. I'd forced my father to bring me on the *Reprisal*, and maybe none of this would have happened if I had stayed home or gone to Aunt Louise. Nonsense, I told myself. Nonsense!

"Cook be makin' Salmagundi," Red said. "It's to cheer us up, like."

"What is Sala, whatever?" I tapped my flute against my canvas shirt to remove any spit that was hiding there. And in spite of my chaotic thoughts I realized that I would see William at the food table. Immediately my nervous fluttering came back. I wondered if he knew about the Burmese Sunrise. How I wished I could talk to him.

"Salmagundi's a treat," Red went on. "Special, like." He set his fiddle in its case so carefully, so gently, tucking a bit of velvet around it, nestling it in the hollowed out space the way he always did. I'd watched him perform this routine a few dozen times. Then he loosened his fiddle bow and slid it into its pegs. Such a fat, round, grimy little pirate! But he loved his fiddle the way I loved my flute.

"What's in Salmagundi?" I asked again. I was not really interested but it seemed a safe subject and something else for me to think on besides the ruby, my guilt, and William.

"Ah!" Red licked his lips. "There's turtle and fish and pork and ham and duck and pigeon and goat and chicken."

I put my hands over my face. "Not one of our chickens? Not Daisy... or Pansy."

Red grinned. "Naw. It's not their time yet. We keeps them till we run out of the salted stuff. Cook chops them all together an' puts in mangos, or oranges, and onions and eggs and cabbage palms and pickled herrings, if'n he has any, and he sprinkles it with hot mustard and garlic and adds a cup or two of vinegar and oil." He looked around. "See? All the men be hurryin'. They knows what's waitin'. Shake a leg, laddie, we wants to get our share." He glanced at me over his shoulder. "There might be beer, too. Sometimes, when we've had deaths and a wheen of woundings, Cap'n orders beers for all."

He set off at a trot, his fiddle safe under his arm, and I trailed behind, stepping around the drying clothes.

It looked like the whole crew was crowding cook and his big stew pot. In between their heads I could see William's bright yellow hair on the other side of the ladling table.

What would he say to me?

There was a pleasant, savory smell that was quite appetizing.

Red elbowed me forward. "Let the boy in," he shouted at the crush of men, but then, right next to me I smelled that vile stench. It overruled the good waft of Salmagundi. A big hand shoved me back, gripping my arm so tight and twisting it so fiercely that I gasped.

"Who are you shovin', you snivelin' pup?" Herc snarled. "I've a good mind to throw you to the sharks. Get ye to the back where ye belongs."

Beside him, Hopper grinned a slobbery grin.

Herc had a bowlful of steaming Salmagundi in each hand, one of which I supposed he was carrying for Hopper. I swung around and my elbow slammed against Herc's, spilling the scalding Salmagundi over his bare legs and feet and onto the deck.

Herc yowled and dropped both bowls.

"Dogblast it, ye scurvy monkey. Ye did that apurpose!"

He was dancing, lifting one leg and then the other, blowing on one hand to cool it where the stew had splashed.

"I'm sorry," I said. "I didn't mean it to happen."

Herc grabbed a bowl out of the hand of a pirate called Wolf and I could see, before he lifted his arm, that his intention was to throw it over me.

I pushed as hard as I could against his chest, and at the same time Wolf howled, "Let go o' that, ye thievin' dog. That's me dinner ye have there!"

I saw Wolf reach up and grab the bowl to wrest it from Herc and its contents landed on the deck, too.

Wolf was crouched, spoon scraping the pile of scalding Salmagundi back into his bowl, cursing Herc with pirate curses that by now were all familiar to me.

"Who are you callin' a stinkin' putrifyin' cur?" Herc yelled at Wolf.

"Go smell yerself," Wolf yelled back. "You're a putrifyin' cur that's been dead..."

Red grabbed me to pull me away. "It'll be ragin' in a minute," he muttered.

Then a shot was fired, and a voice called, "Enough! Get over this lunacy, or there'll be the cat for all of yez."

It was my father. Standing beside him was Mr. Trimble, holding his pistol.

The cat-o'-nine-tails. That threat was enough to slow things down.

"Don't be frettin'," Red whispered to me. "He shot it over the side, that's all. 'Twas to get our attention."

"Cook has made more than enough stew," my father said. "Come ye over in an orderly manner and get it. And be quick about it. There're burials to attend to after yez eat."

Perhaps it was my father's voice and demeanor or the reminder of the dead sailors that cooled the men. We still crowded the table and the Salmagundi pot but there was less frenzy now.

"It'll be forgot before they've done eatin'," Red assured me. "Pay nobody no mind."

I saw William then, for the first time since what I'd come to think of as my "revelation."

His eyes met mine. I thought his look was different now. More aware, with something in it of shyness. I also thought I might be seeing what I wanted to see.

He filled up my bowl.

"Thank ye," I said.

"I gave ye the best pieces," he said.

And I moved on.

Red and I sat at the long wooden table to eat. The weather was better. No rain, just gloomy clouds hanging over the ship. The men were quiet, gloomy too, with the reminder that they had shipmates to bury.

When I looked along the table I saw Herc. He was bent over, spreading something on his legs and feet.

"Goose fat," Red said. "Cook keeps some for when one of us needs it. Don't ye worry, laddie. Herc'll not be going after ye on the *Reprisal*. He's too conversant with the Code, same as the rest of us. Course..." he licked his bowl, slurping up the remains of his Salmagundi. "Course, on shore ye'd do well to mind yerself."

I nodded. "I know."

Red peered into my empty bowl. "Ye want me to finish that for ye?"

"There's nothing left," I said.

"There's a lick or two still."

The rain had started again and the black clouds above the ship were bloated with more rain to come.

Nice day for a burial.

Chapter Twelve

Rain spouted down, slashing off the deck, leveling the sea. The three bodies, sewn into shrouds made from old sails, lay side by side. The men huddled around them. I looked for William and saw him toward the back. I saw Herc. He mouthed something at me. I didn't know what, and I was glad.

Hopper stood with me and Red. There would be music, after.

My father and Mr. Trimble stood pole straight by the railing. The rain eased, and stopped. Clouds still threatened but my father opened the Bible he held. I presumed it to be the one I had seen on the shelf of the cupboard in his cabin. His finger marked a page. He opened the book at that place and began to read.

The words were from a psalm that I knew. It spoke of walking through the valley of death and fearing no evil. I glanced every now and then at the faces around me. They were solemn and attentive, which surprised me. My father spoke reverentially of those who had drowned while doing their duty as pirates, and then closed with a prayer. Some of the men joined in. I supposed they had lived ordinary lives before they became pirates. They might have attended church, been taken by mothers to Bible school. I had noticed that some of them wore holy medallions or crosses that gleamed and glittered on bare chests. One wore a Jewish star. Many of the men made the sign of the cross as soon as the prayer was finished, and then we all bowed our heads as Ike and Jonty came forward and, one by one, slid the canvas-shrouded bodies over the railing.

"We commit their bodies to the sea," my father said.

I heard no sound, not even a splash as the sea took them.

There was a small lull afterward.

Then Mr. Trimble shouted, "There's work to be done, men. Get to it."

Even though the rain came and went the men worked

and we played. Two or three times Hopper snarled at me that I wasn't "keepin' up with the tune." Once his crutch tripped me as I took a step forward.

"Watch where ye be goin', ye hen-hearted numbskull!" he yelled.

I kept on playing.

⚓

The rain cleared away entirely the next day and the clothes on the deck began steaming and giving off foul odors, even though they were now supposed to be clean.

The wet had left a legacy of coughs and phlegm that was hacked up and spat and usually missed going over the railing. You had to watch where you stepped. Pew's remedies did no good.

There was a plague of fleas below decks and arms and legs and necks were spotted with red and oozing bites. The ship was filled with the smells of burning pitch and brimstone designed to kill off the pestilence.

"Them lice likes the stuff we gives them," Red said. "'Tis mother's milk to them."

There were beetles and cockroaches by the thousands. They got into blankets and bedrolls and their tramped-on corpses littered the deck. The deck was washed down with vinegar to keep them at bay but nothing did any good.

Meantime, the men worked, and lazed. When there was little work to be done they were bored. The cards came out and the dice. They wanted music and they liked to sing as they played cards and a game called "Flick" whose rules seemed to change by the minute.

I had little chance to talk to William. And I was guilty that I hadn't told my father William was now privy to my secret identity. I did not know my father, the pirate captain, the way I had known him in my other life, so I was unsure how he would react. And what about the Burmese Sunrise? Best to stay quiet about that and about William's sharing of my secret. "I'll not be telling," he had said. I would not be telling either.

I did have minutes with him now and then, minutes when we were alone. I treasured them and played them over and over in my mind. I felt sure I took meanings from them that weren't there, so anxious was I to discover some tender feelings for me in the words he spoke.

There were two occasions, though, that I had played back so often they were getting dog-eared, the way a page does when you read it over and over.

Standing together, looking over the railing one sun-sparkled day when a little breeze blew and ruffed the sails of the *Reprisal*, William said, without looking at me,

"How long was yer hair afore ye cut it to come aboard?"

He didn't turn toward me as I answered, my heart pounding. "It reached my waist. Soon I would have been wearing it up."

He nodded and I stood, stupidly atremble, looking at his smooth brown shoulder, so close to mine. If I'd wanted to I could have turned and brushed it with my lips. I did want to, but I couldn't.

Another day, a stormy day with gray sky and gray sea he looked at me and said, "Yer eyes are the same color as the sea, when it storms like this. Did ye know that?"

"No." I said, "I did not know that."

Afterward I thought of so many other answers I could have given, such as, "And your eyes are as blue as the sea with the sun on it." But I would not have dared.

One day the lookout called a sail. There was excitement on the *Reprisal*. The sighted ship was a brigantine, two-masted, flying what Red said was a Cuban flag. Her name was the *Auguste*. We followed her for several days, then raised the Jolly Roger, came up beside her and fired a shot across her bow. Red, Hopper, and I pounded out our loud music while our crew did their vaporing, which made me think again of some heathen Hottentot dance. It seemed the Skull and Crossbones flag, the cannon shot, the vaporing, and the music had together filled the sailors of the other ship with terror.

They surrendered immediately.

The *Reprisal* crew was so enraged when they found no gold or coins in the *Auguste*, that they wanted to scuttle her right away and shoot her crew. "Fer wastin' our time, ye stinkin' dogs."

I could easily imagine how they had wanted to torture and kill my father's friend, Captain Brigham.

The *Auguste's* captain apologized for providing so little of interest to us. Tempers lightened when he admitted to having three hogsheads of French brandy hidden in the hold, so our men took those and the crew's clothes, a compass, a barrel of potatoes, two fine suits of clothes belonging to the captain, and two powdered wigs.

The brandy, opened as soon as they were back on the *Reprisal*, was swigged with gusto. I saw that my father swigged his share, but that after a short while he and Mr. Trimble left for the wheelhouse. I saw that William drank from a cup that he topped up with water. How much brandy, if any, was already in the cup I had no way of knowing. The pirates called for music, but Red and Hopper were both besotted and complained that this time they wanted to be left in peace to drink their fill, so the crew sang and danced with one another without benefit of music.

"Boy! Young pup!" That was Herc and he was calling to me. His words slurred in a drunken fashion and when he tried to stand he slithered back down. He had purloined one of the powdered wigs and he looked so foolish that for a minute I wanted to laugh.

"Somebody give the whelp a tot of this 'ere good brandy," he shouted. "I'd see to it meself, but I'm not fit."

He tried again to stand.

"Let the boy be." That was Red and the voice was just as drunken, but there was affection in it and in the inebriated smile he gave me.

I decided it was time for me to leave.

The night was beautiful. Moon lay in a silver stripe across the sea. I looked up and saw a shooting star that hurled itself down to touch the tip of our mainmast. What should I wish for? I knew, and felt a sudden warmth creep across my body. Leaning across the railing I watched the phosphorescence that sailed alongside our ship. The faint drunken singing and shouts of the crew drifted toward me and I thought how happy they sounded. I thought how three of their friends, just a few days past, had gone down to Davy's Locker.

I thought of William.

And that was when I heard soft footsteps behind me.

It seemed right that it would be William in this place at this time and I turned dreamily around.

But it was not William.

Chapter Thirteen

I smelled him before I saw him, that sweet, rotten perfume coming along the shadowy deck toward me.

He was holding a cup of brandy and I could smell it, too, on him and as it splashed over on the deck. He still wore the powdered wig, lopsided on his huge, round head. But it didn't make me want to laugh now. I was terrified.

"Here, laddie, I brought you your share. You be a man now, and a priatt..." He stumbled over the word, trying to say "pirate."

I wanted to back away, but I couldn't. I remembered the rats being forced to drink, the way they were swung by their tails and tossed into the ocean.

He grabbed my arm and I struck at his face with my fist and hammered on his bulbous nose with my flute. "Get away! Get away!"

"Ha! You think I come all this way... all this lonely..." He stopped to belch. "...all this lonely way so ye could refuse my gest..." Belch. "...gesture of kindness?"

We were wrestling. I reached for his hair but it was the wig and it came off in my hand.

"Hey! Ye ungrate ... ungrateful, stinkin' sprog!" He had his arm around my waist, forcing me back against the railing, pushing the rim of the dripping cup against my clenched teeth. Some dribbled into my mouth and I spat it at his face. Now he had a beefy arm around my chest. Suddenly he stopped talking and his hands moved across my bosoms and he seemed suddenly not so drunk as he said, "What's this? What am I feelin' here? By God's tooth, you be a wench, a wench. Forsooth, I haven't touched a wench since we sailed out of Port Teresa."

I struggled with all my might.

But he had the hem of the canvas shirt and he was trying to pull it up as I struggled to keep it down. He and his smell were all over me and I kicked and screamed and suddenly there was William and he was pulling Herc away from me. But Herc was too strong, drunk as he was. I saw William reach down where a piece of timber lay, ragged at the edges, and he lifted it and thumped it into the back of Herc's head.

Herc grunted and stumbled to his knees. The cup of brandy fell with a clatter.

Blood, black as tar in the pale light, ran down his forehead and into his eyes. He pushed himself onto all fours, then pulled himself the rest of the way with the help of the railing.

William raised the timber again but Herc wrestled with him, his weight and reach so much greater than William's, and soon he had wrenched it from his hand.

William stood in front of me, shielding me.

"Boy," Herc said and I wondered how he could be so coherent when he'd been so drunk before.

"There will be consequences for this, me lad. Ye'd best start in on yer prayers. And you!" His bloodied head poked forward toward me. "I'll be makin' use of what I learned this night, good Miss. You can lay to that."

He lifted the wig, held it to his head to stop the flow of blood, and staggered back the way he had come.

Chapter Fourteen

*W*illiam and I stood facing each other. I was shaking so much I had to hold on to his arm.

"Are ye all right?"

"No," I said. "I feel sick. What will he do? And my father... I promised him." I fought hard to keep back the sob that was choking me, but it came and when it did William put his arms tight around me and held me against him. I could feel his heart beating and the smoothness of his shoulder against my cheek. How could I be aware of such things when my father and I were both in mortal danger?

He held me a little away from him as if he, too,

remembered the enormity of Herc's discovery.

"He'll tell the others," I said.

"Aye. I fear he will. I doubt yer father'll be able to help ye. But ye must tell him. Ye must tell him now afore it gets out. I'll go wi' ye. We'll go portside so as not to pass the crew."

"No. I want to tell him alone."

"Then I'll go wi' ye part of the way."

I stooped and picked up my flute where it had rolled to a corner of the deck. "I poked him hard with this," I said and managed a smile. "On his nose."

We walked a little apart. I knew that made sense. Herc did not know that the cabin boy also knew me for a girl. He might have been simply protecting me because I was young and his friend. But William had hit him. Somehow, he would have to pay.

We walked in silence. The *Reprisal* swayed lazily side to side, as if she too had partaken of the French brandy. Or as if she'd worked hard enough today and was taking her rest.

I looked up at the mast where the Jolly Roger no longer flew, Skull and Crossbones at the ready. Instead an innocent English ensign drooped from the masthead. The sails made a whispery luffing sound, holding almost no wind. The sky was a dazzle of quiet stars. It was a still and peaceful night, except for the faint merrymaking from the starboard deck and for the turmoil inside of me. Maybe this was the calm before the storm, if indeed a squall was coming. I was remembering my father's warnings and the words of the Code of Conduct. Lashing, keelhauling, marooning! And suddenly I realized I was gasping for breath.

"It'll be all right," William took my hand. "What are ye called?" he asked.

"Catherine."

He nodded. "'Tis a name I've always fancied."

In spite of everything I was pleased.

Something small and silent rubbed against my legs. "Daisy," I whispered and I rubbed the little goat's head. "Don't be close to me, my love. It's not safe."

I was speaking to Daisy but to William, too.

"We'll take you back to be with Pansy," I told her.

She walked beside us as we took her as far as her open pen.

My father was in his cabin but there was someone with him. We could hear voices, whispering voices. His cabin door would be open, of course and... and then I smelled Herc's smell.

William caught my arm and we stood absolutely still. The words came to us, the furtive, secretive words.

Fleetingly I thought of how I'd so often eavesdropped on my father and Mr. Trimble at home. How daring I'd felt. This now, this was life-or-death listening.

"Ye've got what I want," Herc said, "If ye gives it to me I'll keep me mouth shut and there'll be no more made of the matter. No mention of the girl."

I heard my father's voice, firm and uncompromising. "I give ye my word. The Burmese Sunrise is in my house, back in Port Teresa. It will be yours at the end of the cruise. If ye do as ye say and keep yer mouth shut. But I swear to ye, ye'll never see it and never find it, if ye break yer promise...."

"Ah now, 'twill be hard. I like a young lass. I've a notion to get to know her better, in her new state as it were."

Beside me William twitched and took a small step toward the open door.

I seized his arm.

"One move toward her and I'll cut yer throat, Herc," my father said quite graciously. "Twill give me pleasure."

"Remember, Cap'n. If I *do* tell, ye'll be bloodied too." The satisfaction in Herc's voice told me he was savoring this.

"If ye do tell, there'll be no Burmese Sunrise," my father said. "Make yer choice."

It was time. I drew William a few more steps away

from the open door and whispered. "Please go now. I want to do this alone."

He did not argue.

⚓

My father and Herc stopped talking as I walked into the cabin.

"Did yer protector not come wi' ye?" Herc asked. Blood had caked on his forehead and there was more, dried around his nose. My doing, I thought with satisfaction.

My father laid his arm across my shoulders. "Are you all right, Charlie?"

"Charlie! Charlie!" Herc sneered. "Now there's a name for a God-fearin' young lady!"

"We have made our deal," my father said. "Leave!"

"Not so fast." Herc fingered his nose, felt around his head where the black blood was matted in his eyebrow. "There's another vexin' matter to be considered." His eyes narrowed. "That mangy dog of a cabin boy did this. I want him punished. He attacked another crewman, near knocked the brains out o' me, walloped me on me head here."

"He was..." I began and realized that I should not finish what I had started to say. That William was defending me from Herc's unseemly attentions. To do that William would have had to know I was a girl. I did not want him in more trouble.

"The mangy cur has to pay. Ye understands that, Cap'n. He swore the oath, same as the rest of us."

"He didn't use a knife," I said quickly. "The Code spoke of a knife."

Herc narrowed his eyes. "'Tis the same as if he did. His intent was to kill me."

How could he be so sober, so fast, I wondered.

"I understand," my father said, and I understood, also. William had to pay the price too for Herc's silence.

"So ye'll agree, then? It's the cat for the boy?"

"No," I shouted.

Herc poked his eyebrow and dried flakes of blood sprinkled onto his shoulder.

My father nodded.

The nod pierced my heart.

Chapter Fifteen

I didn't see William again that night but I went to the fo'c's'le in search of Mr. Trimble. As quartermaster he would be in charge of administering the punishment.

"Can't you stop it?" I pleaded. I didn't cry because I was still a pirate, even if a reluctant one.

"It's not possible, Catherine... I mean... Charlie." He paused. "The lad broke the rule. I will try to go as easy on him as possible without revealing my intentions to the crew. If I did, questions would be asked. That would be dangerous for you and the cap'n."

"I don't care," I said.

But I had to care.

I slept little and in the morning, when I went on deck, I was still pretending to myself that something would have changed. Somehow William would escape the cat. I'd never seen it in use. I'd heard of it, though. I'd heard it spoken with as much dread as a pirate allowed himself to show. I walked slowly, giving more time for a change of mind, which I truly knew would never come.

The sky had darkened again and I felt the beginnings of a squall. The *Reprisal* rocked drunkenly. Lines banged against the masts. Raindrops, big and round, splashed on the deck. I smelled the spilled French brandy from the night before.

If there were a storm, would it still happen?

"Hurry up, ye lazy mutt," Hopper called to me. "Ye don't want to miss it." He grinned his horrible grin and looked over my shoulder. "Seems like ye're just in time."

I saw William then, stripped to the waist, barefoot, coming along the deck. Harry Ho and Stipe walked like jailers, one on either side of him. Men stood around, not working, waiting.

Herc lounged by the rail, picking at his teeth. He had a red scarf around his head, just like the one my father had bought for me on that day, so long ago, when we'd set out from home to be pirates. He leered at me when I glanced in his direction, and pursed his lips in a fake kiss.

The gesture made me shudder. How was I going to deal with him, now that he knew? He would be wary of my father and careful not to reveal my identity. But the *Reprisal* had many dark corners.

I saw Mr. Trimble. He carried a sailcloth bag. A whisper went around the small crowd, a shivery whisper.

My blood chilled. Inside that bag was the cat-o'-nine-tails.

I wet my lips and swallowed the claw in my throat.

Red came to stand beside me.

"No need for ye to watch, lad," he whispered. "It be an unpleasant sight and I'll lay to that."

Behind us Hopper cackled.

My father came striding along, grim faced. How could he let this happen? I'd always loved him so much. Not now. Not anymore.

I turned my back to William. I remembered that he was suffering this because of me. Because he had tried to save me from Herc. Because he had kept my secret.

I would watch. That would be my share of the punishment.

He half lay across the railing, his hand gripping the

top bar, his knuckles white and shining.

Someone was yelling, "I seen it! I swear on Blackbeard's ghost. I seen it."

The crowd parted and I recognized the man. He was One-Eyed Jack, who sometimes wore a black shade over the puckered pit where his eye had once rested, and sometimes didn't. Today the patch was in place.

"Ne'er heard tell o' no albatross in these parts. They fly south, down by the southern shore."

"I tell you I seen it."

"You got only one eye, mate. You was seein' what wasn't there."

"Or ye were drunk." There was some half-hearted laughter.

"I seen it." Jack's voice quavered. "It come out o' the clouds yonder." He pointed, and heads lifted to scan the dark sky.

"Ye knows about albatross," Jack went on, his voice still quavering. "They holds the souls o' dead sailors. Or foretell bad luck. That albatross fixed his eyes on the *Reprisal,* and his wings..." Jack held out his arms. "The wings on him near touched our mainmast."

"You be blatherin', ye fool," Fish told him. "None o' the rest o' us seen him."

But there was an uneasy shuffling around and secret

glances at the sky.

"We needs to be gettin' on with the whippin'," Herc yelled. "Get ye started, Quarter!"

"Don't you see?" I yelled. "The albatross was telling you it would be bad luck to whip William. Something bad could happen to the ship, or to you."

I knew about pirate superstitions. If I could move their attention away from William...

"If'n there was an albatross he knew nothin' of whippin' or of this here cabin boy," Herc said. "Do what you need to do, Quarter."

Mr. Trimble opened the bag and pulled out the cat.

The albatross wasn't going to stop them. Nothing was going to stop them. I closed my eyes and made myself open them again. Rain pelted me, ran down my neck and into my shirt.

Mr. Trimble hefted the whip in his hand, feeling the weight of it. He spat on his palm, paused, then drew back his arm and the whip, with its long, braided leather tails cracked down on William's back.

A sigh, like a wind, swept through the small crowd.

"I seen the albatross," One-Eyed Jack yelled but now no one was listening.

The rain was falling faster, falling on William's bare back. Already I could see the red stripes fanning across it.

I found myself counting them. Nine red welts, raw and bleeding.

Mr. Trimble's arm stretched back and the whip whistled down again.

You promised, you promised, I thought. You promised me you would not lash him so hard.

My eyes flickered toward Herc. He was watching me. My father? His face never changed, stern and unemotional.

William! Now the ugly bleeding stripes crisscrossed on his back, like the paths in the maze game I sometimes played with my mother. Find your way out! I called to him silently. But there was no way out.

How could William not scream? How could there be such quiet. Inside he must be screaming.

Mr. Trimble's arm went back a third time. The cat's tails were darkened with blood.

"Stop!" I yelled and I leaped forward and wrenched the handle of the cat from Mr. Trimble's hand. It was wet, with rain or sweat or blood.

In that second I saw Mr. Trimble's shocked face. I felt the silence and then heard the shouts of the men. I had no idea what they were shouting. I swung the cat, my only thought to throw this cruel thing over the railing into the sea.

Someone had caught me from behind. A hand wrestled

the cat from my grip and it fell on the deck, the tails still moving angrily.

My father. I was pressed against him, my back against his belly, his voice whispering in my ear. "No, Catherine. No."

Now I could hear the shouts of the men even louder and I knew every word they called out.

"Is the boy mad?"

"What do ye think ye're doin', ye impudent dog?"

"Lash him, too. Give him the cat, the pair of 'em together."

Then I heard Red's voice, reasoning. "There be nothin' in the Code as says ye gets a punishment for trying to stop a lashin'. The lad got shattered at what he was seein'. He be young..."

"Makes no difference. He needs a lashin' fer his meddlin'."

My father's arms tightened at my waist.

Two men rushed toward us. One was Perry, the other Gil. Gil reached out for me. I saw his arm as if through a spyglass. I'd watched that whale tattoo take shape, the gunpowder flaming under his skin. "It be a humpback whale," he'd told me. "They be travelers, like me." And he'd smiled at me as if we were friends and shipmates.

Perry seized one of my shoulders. He reached for

the front of my shirt, pulled me toward him and I heard the rip, the tearing sound of the burlap. I grabbed it and tried to hold it tight against me, but it half fell away, in a flap, and I knew before the yelling began that I had been discovered.

"Hound's breath! She be a girl."

"And a likely one!"

There were catcalls and obscene observations and cursing and then, through it I heard, clearly, "She be our bad luck! She brung it wi' her. If it hasn't hit us full speed yet, 'twill."

And then One-Eyed Jack, screaming out the words, "The albatross. The albatross knew. The *Reprisal* is destroyed. We'll all be drowned and our ship wi' us."

"The cap'n knew." I didn't know who said that but it caused a sudden quiet.

"Get rid of her and let her ill luck go wi' her. Throw her to the sharks. And throw the cap'n over as well."

"Not so fast." That was Herc. He'd come close. His smell made my stomach churn. "Pity to waste the lass. She be a likely lookin' one."

William was up on all fours, dragging himself toward me. I'd wanted the lashing to stop but not this way.

I clutched the pieces of burlap in front of me. If my father had not still been holding me I would have fallen.

Terror filled me. I was not brave, like William.

And then my father's arms dropped away.

He was letting them have me! Sobs that I tried to hide choked me. Would I be lashed with the cat-o'-nine-tails? Or thrown to the sharks? Or, heaven help me, thrown to the pirates?

There was Herc again. "Leave the cap'n to me. I'll make certain he gets what he deserves, the lyin' dog."

Oh, my poor father! Herc would go to any lengths to discover where the Burmese Sunrise was. I had no notion of what he would do to my father but I knew it would be savage and merciless. He would get the whereabouts of the Burmese Sunrise. My poor father. I had made him bring me. And this was how it would all end. He shouted to be heard.

"Don't lay a hand on her. Any of you. Catherine..."

There were sniggerings of "Catherines" from the crew and a surge toward us that stopped as suddenly as it had begun.

I turned and saw that my father was standing over Gil and that he had his cutlass in his hand.

"Catherine. Get ye behind me," he ordered.

I moved quickly.

"Easy, Cap'n. What good does it do ye to harm any one of us?"

That was Herc, his voice oily and soothing. "Put away your cutlass and..."

There was a scraping sound and then an oath and I saw Hopper behind my father. Even as I watched he brought his crutch down with a crash on my father's head.

My father turned sideways and Hopper hit him again, knocking him over.

There was a dull crash and then a sharper bang.

My father had fallen. His head hit the rim of the half barrel of rain water, still standing since the storm. Water sloshed onto the deck and lap, lap, lapped across my father's face as he lay there bleeding.

Chapter Sixteen

My father was dying on the deck of his ship. His eyes were closed, his body limp. It wasn't the blow that had killed him. When he fell he hit his head on the rim of the water barrel.

No crewmember spoke or moved.

In the silence I heard the sea breathing around us and beneath us. I saw the water in the barrel ripple to a stop.

Then One-Eyed Jack shouted, "I told yez I seen the albatross. I told yez."

"Hold yer tongue, ye crazy baboon," Fish yelled.

"I seen it," Jack muttered.

I ran forward and knelt by my father.

"Father! Oh please, Father. Open your eyes. I'm here. Open your eyes."

Hopper was talking loud and angry. "I had to stop him. Yez all saw. He was goin' to slash Gil. Came at him with his cutlass. Cap'n or not, he needed stoppin'. No fault o' mine. 'Twas his own fallin' that killed him."

"Stop yer jibberin'," Herc said. "Nobody's puttin' blame on you."

The pirates crowded around. I saw William, stumbling toward us, moving crablike, and I saw that Herc was shoving everyone aside, yelling, "All o' yez, stand back."

I was murmuring and I didn't know if my father could hear me. "I'm sorry I was so strong-willed. I should have listened to you. Can you forgive me?"

I touched my father's cheek and he smiled the weakest of smiles. He lifted his hand and made a movement that told me he wanted me to come closer and I saw he was trying to form words but there was blood in his mouth.

Red gave me a bowl of water and I wet my finger and ran it along my father's lips.

"Sell," he whispered. I thought it was "sell." Another word, coming, foaming in his mouth "Far..." he said and tried for more but there was too much blood now and whatever else he tried to say was only a blur.

Herc pushed himself between us and shouted at my

father.

"I kept my word. I said naught about the wench. Ye owe me, Cap'n. If the men knew ye brought yer girl on the ship ye both would have been murdered. I saved ye. So where is it? Where is it?"

William tugged at Herc's leg and Herc slapped him away.

My father's eyes were closed.

My tears fell, hot and stinging, on his dear face. "My beloved father," I whispered.

Someone yelled, "He be finished. Cap'n's gone."

"No," I whispered, and then, suddenly, my father's eyes opened again and he said distinctly, "Maggie."

His last word, my mother's name.

His head rolled to the side and I knew then it was over.

The silence was broken by a loud voice. Herc's! Herc standing almost astride my dead father.

"Cap'n be dead. Who among us will be cap'n now?" His face was filled with rage. "Bad cess to his soul! Till the end he broke his word to me. I was to get what I wanted and he didn't give it!"

He spat on the deck. "Yer vote, men? Who among us'll be cap'n now."

"I say, Herc McDonald!"

"But was I hearin' right? Did ye know about the witch?"

I thought that was Bear who asked.

"I guessed it. I was goin' to tell yez all after the floggin'. Thought 'twould be amusin' for us all to find out, for sure, together." He leered at me and made obscene gestures at the men. "But there's no time for play. We needs to throw her off this ship afore somethin' worse happens."

"Aye."

"Aye."

"Give me a show o' hands, then. Who among us'll be cap'n now? Yer vote? If ye wants it to be me, show me yer hands."

Hands were raised, a thicket of them.

"Ye be cap'n now, Herc."

"'Tis you."

Herc's teeth flashed as he smiled.

"So t'will be. Another vote then? What shall we do with the wench and the scurrilous dog that took the whip to keep her secret. He wasn't goin' to share her, and ye can lay to that. Tried to silence me, to boot. I say we maroon 'em both."

"Aye. Maroon them."

"Put her off, and the pus-filled pup with her."

"Pox Island, that be the place," Herc shouted. "We pass alongside it afore nightfall. They'll be thrown ashore and that'll be the end o' them. Good riddance, I say."

"Good riddance!"

"We must first bury the Cap'n," Mr. Trimble said, but weakly, and I knew he was afraid for himself. Afraid it would be discovered that he'd known about me too and kept his silence. Perhaps he was afraid now that I would give him away. Mr. Trimble! I'd always thought him a strong man. But how could I blame him? His confession of knowledge would serve no purpose and would lead to marooning for him too. I supposed that when faced with such a death even a brave man could become a coward. I knew that if I had a way out for William and me, even a cowardly way, I would take it.

"A burial he shall have," Herc announced. "Take his feet, Fish. Gil, take his head. Swing him up and over the side."

"Wait!" I seized Gil's arm. "Can't we sew him in a shroud? Can't we say some holy words before..."

"Say yer own words, ye accursed wench! Heave him over, lads!"

I ran to the railing as my father's body was balanced between the two pirates and hurled into the sea.

I did say my own words, the same ones that my father and I together had arranged to have on my mother's tombstone. William stood beside me, holding tight to the rail to keep himself erect, and just as my father's body disappeared beneath the waves I heard the faint strains of a violin in the distance. It was a mournful melody and I knew it was Red, paying his own respects to his old captain. It was Red who passed us by and casually dropped a shirt across William's shoulders.

Pox Island was a dot on the horizon that came closer as the wind filled our sails.

William and I huddled by the port rail, watching as the bare rock came closer and closer. Speed lifted ice-cold spray that lashed our faces. Beside us, Gil stood guard.

"Does he think we're goin' to escape?" William asked.

"Perhaps he suspects we might swim for our lives, all the way to Pox Island." I made my voice light though there was nothing but heaviness and despair inside of me. What did I care about anything? My father was dead.... my own darling father.

"Best we should wait for our ride," William said and I suspected his ordinary voice was false and put on for me.

I'd asked Gil's permission to get some goose grease from cook for the gashes in William's back but he'd shaken his head. "Ye gets no kindnesses from any o' us, ye deceivin' fishwife," he said.

I took William's hand in mine. "All of this is my fault," I said. "You did nothing but keep your counsel when you found my secret. I am sorry with all my heart. It should be only me taking the punishment. Not you. Not my father." My throat choked with more tears that I wouldn't allow my eyes to shed. "Look what I've done."

"Would I let ye face this alone?" William asked. "Never. We'll finish it together."

I smelled Herc then and I saw him coming toward us.

"I'm takin' the girl," he told Gil.

"No!" William lunged at Herc but he was thrown back against the bulwark and Gil had a knife to his neck. "Stay where ye are and pay a mind to the cap'n," Gil grunted.

Herc pulled on my arm, hauling me behind him along the deck like a sack of grain.

We stopped. His grip loosened. "On yer feet, girl. You and me's goin' to exchange words."

He pulled me close, the smell of him repulsing me.

"This be yer last chance, girl." His face was pushed so close to mine I could see the blackheads buried in his skin and the thick, wiry hairs that grew out of his nose.

"Where is the Burmese Sunrise?"

"I don't know."

"Tell me and it'll go easier on ye."

"I don't know."

"Tell me what he said, there, when he was goin' to face his maker."

"You heard, same as me," I said.

"Made no more sense than a seal's barkin'. Tell me the words again."

"He said, 'Sell' and something like 'Far.' And then my mother's name."

"Sell? He's tellin' you to sell the Burmese. That speckle-shirted dog! Them's the words I thought I heard. If ye knows where that ruby be and ye plans on sellin'..."

"I don't. I don't know anything."

He shook me till I thought my head would fall off. "Ye know. Ye know right well."

"I don't." The words rattled out of me. "I... I don't. I have no need for the Burmese Sunrise. I have more need for my life. Don't you think I would be willing?"

"I'm goin' to lash the skin off yer back afore I maroon ye! I'm goin' to tie ye to the mast and let the men cut ye, cut ye a hundred times. Ye'll be beggin' to be throwed in the sea along wi' yer father when we be finished wi' ye."

I felt myself sway. My mind lurched. I fell forward.

"Ah, ye be ignorant as me!" He kicked my stomach so my breath gushed out of me.

"Get ye away. We'll be at the island afore the hour's up."

I muttered words.

He bent to hear, hope struggling in his face along with anger. "Are ye' preparin' to tell me?

"I'm preparing to tell you, you stink," I said. "You smell like a dead pig!"

He kicked me again but I didn't care. I savored the small triumph of disparaging him.

I dragged myself up then, wheezing, holding on to my stomach, gasping for the breath that had blown out of me and when I looked across the sea I saw that we had reached Pox Island.

Chapter Seventeen

The anchor smashed down, down, down and the *Reprisal* shuddered as it caught in the bottom of the ocean.

Ike and Fish and Barton and Turkey, four of the burliest of the pirates, lowered the wooden rowboat into the sea. It thumped against the hull, lurching drunkenly till it bobbed on the water.

It was a big rowboat, the same one that had ferried the fruit and barrels of water aboard before we left Cannon Cove. I remembered my father saying, "It's not too late, Catherine. You can change your mind and leave the next time the boat is rowed ashore." If only I had! Now I was being rowed ashore to an end I could not even imagine.

A rope was hung over the *Reprisal*'s side. Three pirates scrambled down it, sure-footed and nimble.

"Get yez after them!" Herc gave me a shove and I saw how roughly he fisted William's back, pushing him forward.

I went down the rope first, William after me.

We dangled precariously as we scraped down, hand over hand, banging again and again against the lurching hull of the ship.

There were catcalls and laughter as we fell into the rowboat. A box was dropped in beside us. "'Tis food and water, enough for a day or two, and that only from the goodness of me heart," Herc yelled.

"Or so they die slower," Ike yelled. "Aarg! 'Twill be no party ye'll be havin' there on Pox Island."

Their voices drifted clearly on the rain-washed air.

Hopper threw my flute so it clipped the side of my head. It almost fell in the heaving water but I caught it. "Here, girlie. Ye can play yerselves a tune while ye waits fer what's comin'."

I held it and looked up at the circle of men, hanging across the railing above us. There was little pity in the faces. Only Red and Cook, standing a bit apart from the rest, looked grieved. Mr. Trimble had not come to see us off. I had not expected more.

Someone shouted, "Ain't they supposed to have a bottle o' rum and a cutlass wi' them? Ain't that in the rules of maroonin'?"

"There be no rules for maroonin'," Herc shouted back. "'Tis Cap'n's word and Cap'n says.... haul away."

"Cap'n?" I recognized Cook's voice now. "I knowed the boy a long while. He was a good help to me. Would ye let me be givin' him a remembrance of the days we cooked together? 'Tis not much. Just a parcel o' hardtack and a bit o' salt beef?"

"Ye can give it. May it sustain them in their time o' need."

His words brought on gales of laughter and cheering.

We swayed and heaved in the swell and my stomach heaved with every toss.

Above us the *Reprisal* loomed, larger than I remembered her. The crew hung over the sides shouting, "Ta TA!" and "Enjoy yerselves," and "Come back soon!" There was much merriment. They pelted us with oranges and someone lobbed eggs, cooked in their shells. Some of what they threw hit us, some fell in the sea, but some dropped into the boat. It seemed to me like a carnival. I had once thought of pirates as swashbuckling and romantic. What a silly, ignorant girl I'd been.

The two rowers were pulling away now. Gil sat facing us, with his hand on the hilt of his cutlass. His eyes never met mine. None of them paid attention as William and I scooped up the oranges and the eggs and a lemon, big as my fist, that had hit Barton on the head and caused him to curse and blaspheme before it rolled to my feet.

And then I saw Daisy's little white head poke through the railings above me and Pansy beside her. The sight of the two little goats was almost too much for me and I feared I would weep. But I knew this to be a time for strength and not weakness. I was my father's daughter. My strength would honor him.

⚓

Pox Island was more brooding the closer we came. Sheer rock face plummeted down to a small ribbon of sand. There were no trees, no scrub grass, nothing but rocks as big as boulders and stark emptiness. The sea washed over the sand in small waves, and I saw how shallow the water was.

The two men shipped their oars and jumped down, grinding the boat onto the sand. Gil held the cutlass aloft, as if expecting a last-minute mutiny.

"Ye needn't be thinkin' of tryin' the other side. There be no other side." Barton said. "Just rock, mateys, just rock."

"Out, the two of yez!" Turkey shouted. "Take your ill

luck with ye, girl. We have no wish for it on our ship. And make haste about it. We be in a hurry."

"Aye, we be goin' places, even if yez are not!"

They chortled at their own humor and I could see they felt no sorrow for our plight as they rowed away, leaving us knee deep in the shore water of Pox Island.

Ike had hurled our precious package of food far up on the rocks. At least they had allowed us that.

We churned our way through the shallow water. Little fishes darted around our ankles.

"We'll catch us some," William promised, but I knew we had no means of doing that except with our hands. I noted how quickly the fish flitted around us. But perhaps they could be caught.

I kept a tight grip on my flute. Maybe I could charm them out of the water with my music. My mother had read me a story once about a ghost flute that magicked the birds down from the trees. My mother, who was lying under the ground on Cob Hill, my father, somewhere in this big, wide ocean, his body moving gently with the tide. My father. My dear father. All my fault.

It was suddenly hard for me to breathe.

And there was the *Reprisal*, still at anchor, and there was the rowboat halfway back to her. As I watched, sick at heart, Ike gave me a cheerful wave.

All kinds of muddled thoughts went through my head. We should have overpowered the men despite Ike and his cutlass. He would have chopped us to pieces. But that might have been easier than what lay ahead for us. We should have fought to stay on the *Reprisal*, never have let them put us off. We should run in the water now, swim, try to reach them, beg, promise. But I knew none of those possibilities had ever existed.

We carried our precious eggs and oranges and the lemon carefully over the strip of beach and piled them in the shade of a rock beside the parcel.

I turned again to look. The *Reprisal* had upped anchor and was on her way. She could still have been the ship of my dreams, sails billowing, red-and-gold dragon pointed at adventures to come. But I knew better now. Now she was my ship of darkness.

"I was the one who caused you to be in this danger," I told William, trying to keep the shake out of my voice. "If I had never..."

He put his fingers across my lips to still my words. "I forgive ye," he said.

We stood by the rocks of Pox Island till the *Reprisal*

was just a toy boat in a pond, heading for the horizon.

In a few minutes she disappeared into the far distance and we were alone.

Chapter Eighteen

When my mother died I felt a terrible grief and emptiness. When my father died, just today, his death happened so fast and so tragically that I was numb and choked with sadness. It had seemed unreal. Now, watching the *Reprisal* sail away, there was only disbelief.

William took my hand.

I felt it, wet from the ocean, calloused from the work on the *Reprisal*. His hand was real, he was real, it was all real.

We laid the fruit and eggs on one of the flat rocks below the cliff and William opened Cook's box. Inside were ten hardtack, a bundle of dried meat tied together with a length of cord, and a wedge of cheese. The cheese had small black specks that might have been dead weevils, the usual accompaniment to food on the *Reprisal*.

"Them's not maggots," William said, holding the cheese close to me for inspection. "This be some kind of special cheese that Cook got when we took a French ship. He don't share it much. He says there's people give a lot of gold for a bit o' this. See?" He smiled and I knew his talk was to keep my mind from following the ship that had vanished into the haze at the edge of our world.

"And look!" At the bottom of the box was a flint, a small tin of grease, a knife with a bone handle and a flask of water.

"I will bless Cook all my life," I said as I held the water flask against my cheek. I heard my own words and wondered how long my life would be.

William picked up the knife. He held it out for me to see. "Cook has made a picture on the handle. 'Tis called scrimshaw and when we're in port he sells what he's carved. Most times he has a whale cut on there, or maybe a mermaid. This one has letters. What does it say?"

I looked. "It says COURAGE."

William nodded. "Most people have need of courage. He likely had this ready to sell."

"I think now it's a message for us," I said.

I wondered if perhaps William could not read and as if he knew my thoughts he said, "I can read simple words. This'un has a strange spellin'."

"Yes," I said, "it has." I was filled then with such affection for him that it was hard not to kiss his cheek. But I put away the thought.

Instead I set the knife on the rock and watched him examine the flint. "I can make us a fire with this if we find somethin' to burn."

"Do you think there'll be water?" I asked. "What's here won't last us long."

He kept his head bent as he said, "We'll have to see." I knew that he didn't expect to find more water on this desolate island. And I knew that without water we would surely die.

He took off his shirt, the one Red had tossed to him, and as he did so he winced. I saw that the shirt was stuck to the red, bloody stripes on his back.

"Oh," I said, putting my hand over my lips. "You must be in pain."

"Not much," he said, and it made me smile to see how offhand he was trying to be, and he smiled, too.

I smoothed some of Cook's grease onto the stripe marks and when I finished William said, "'Tis true. It feels better."

But I saw how pale his face was and how the scar on his cheekbone stood out like a thin red line from eyebrow to ear. Without thinking I ran a finger along it, then stepped back. What was I doing?

"First thing we do is search for water." It seemed he had not even been aware of my caress, for that was what it had been.

I helped him put all our food into Cook's box, "In case of animals," William said. "But I don't think there's life besides ours on Pox Island."

I could see it was not possible to climb the bald dome that was the cliff or to go around it in either direction so we could find out if Barton had spoken the truth. So our search was limited to the rocks at its base and to the small strip of beach.

We searched separately.

"There is dried-out seaweed here. I'll have a try at burnin' it," William called. "And look!" He had found the remains of a bleached-out wooden box, washed high against the cliff. "We can make us a signal fire!"

A small one, I thought, but didn't say.

I was the one who found the water.

There was a hollowed-out rock, smooth and gray, about as big around as the top of a barrel. In its depression was water, no more than a few inches of it, but so clear that it held the reflection of the sky.

I stared at it, voiceless for the moment. Then I yelled, "Over here! Water!"

William came and we stood looking into it, seeing ourselves, knowing that this water could be the difference for us between life and death.

William bent over, put his finger into the little pool, licked it and smiled up at me. "No salt," he said. "Rain. Remember, the storm, the day I saw—" He stopped and stood up. The day he had first discovered I was a girl.

"I remember." I was so exuberant that I flung my arms around him, recalling too late the bleeding stripes on his back.

"Sorry," I muttered, releasing him.

"No need for sorry."

We pulled and gathered as much of the dried seaweed as we could find. It was tough and leathery and made my fingers bleed, but I said nothing. Some of it William hacked with our "Courage" knife. When he tried to light it with the flint there was no fire, only smoke.

"We'll have the wood and this. The smoke is all we'll need," William said. "We'll signal the first sail we see."

It comforted me the way he said that. As if any minute we might look up and see a sloop or a schooner gliding across the sea.

We agreed to keep Cook's water for emergencies and lay flat on our bellies to drink from our small rock pool. Nothing in the world had ever tasted so good.

That day we ate a small portion of the cheese and divided one piece of the dried beef.

"I know this isn't Daisy or Pansy we're eating," I said, thankful that I'd seen them both, alive and well, as we were rowed away from the *Reprisal*.

"Aye," he said. "Them two'll live a while yet."

Poor little helpless creatures, I thought. Destined to be a meal in a pirate stomach.

That night we slept in the shelter of the rocks separate from each other. I lay gazing at the stars, aware of William's presence only a few yards away. He had offered me his shirt to put beneath my head but I had declined. What I wished was that I could lie next to him. But perhaps it was better this way. If we lay closer, my strange new feelings might surface, and instinctively I knew that would be wrong and foolish.

We explored the beach and the rocks more thoroughly the next day. We saw no animals, no birds, no life. But there were life signs. Or were they death signs? Others, marooned, or shipwrecked, had been here before us. There was a rock with markings, lines that we decided had been there to count the passing of days. There had been someone, longing for rescue. How many days? I counted fifteen. Had a ship come and taken them off Pox Island? Was it one person alone, or two, as we were? Had they died here? Fifteen days! I shivered and ran to catch up with William.

We started our own marks on another rock. Too soon there were three and then four, days we had not seen another ship. The boards, no more than kindling, and the seaweed and the flint were ready but there had been no need of a signal.

The cheese was finished. We had eaten four of the hardtack, two of the eggs. My stomach ached with hunger.

On the fourth day I caught a sea crab that had crawled up on the sand.

"I can't eat it raw," I said, after William had smashed it with a rock and removed it from its shell.

"Ye can," William said. "Ye have to. We have to hold on to what we have as long as we can. No fire yet, Catherine. There'll be a ship. But we want to have smoke enough to bring 'em to us." He paused. "You and me, we have lives to live.... after."

We laid bits of crab on a rock to dry out and I ate

them.

They were salty and stringy. My stomach rebelled, but it did not disgorge them. William used our Courage knife to pry hard little shelled creatures, no bigger than beans, from rocks close to the tide. They did not taste like beans and were tough, like morsels of leather.

We finished the last hardtack on the sixth day, and by then we had sucked one of the oranges dry and chewed the peel. There were still six pieces of beef, two oranges and the lemon.

I caught William pretending he had eaten his piece of meat and saving the extra piece for me. "Don't do that," I said. "I want you to live as long as I do. Do you think I want to be left here alone?"

I watched him carefully after that but it didn't happen again.

William caught a fish on the sixth day. We had tried to cup one in our hands as they darted around our feet, but they were too fast. I began to believe they were playing a game with us, a game we never won.

Then William tied a morsel of precious meat on the end of the cord that had been round our sticks of beef and stood patiently for hours on a sea rock, dangling it hopefully into the water. A fish bit. This time I said not a word about eating a raw sea creature, skin and bones as well as flesh. I only hoped he could catch another one.

We were both burned with the never-ending sun, even though when it was highest in the sky we stayed in the shade of the rocks. William's gashes were healing. We bathed, modestly and separately, in the ocean and I thought the salt water had helped cleanse the wounds. Cook's grease soothed them afterward and we scraped the grease tin for our sunburned ears and lips.

We were thirsty, thirsty, thirsty. The small store of rock water was going down and we allowed ourselves only four sips a day. Our lips were dry and cracked and when the grease was gone we had nothing left to soothe them. It was hard to swallow. We found small stones and sucked on them trying to produce some saliva.

I printed my father's dying words with my finger in the sand.

SELL FAR MAGGIE.

I was certain they contained a message for me, a message to tell me where the Burmese Sunrise was hidden. Herc had thought so, too. But what did it mean? I tried putting other words between the ones I had. Putting other words in front of them, after them. Nothing made sense. My poor father's voice had been so blurred and choked with blood. When I remembered those last minutes I thought my heart would break. I printed the words over and over. Then, one evening, when we were staring out at the endless sea, William moved his foot and it touched the curve of the printed S on the SELL I had just written. Suddenly the S looked like a B. BELL.

I stared at it. Bell Beach, where my mother and I had gone so often to gather shells and sea glass. Had my father hidden it there, in such a public place? I looked at the FAR and with my finger changed the first letter to a J. JAR.

I knew. He was telling me the jewel was hidden in the jar of rocks from Bell Beach.

"William," I gasped. "I know what he said." And I told him about the rocks and shells my mother and I had collected during those happy days at Bell Beach and how she had kept them in a jar at the foot of her bed.

"I think, when she was sick, she relived those days," I said, and for a minute my returning grief overshadowed my pleasure at deciphering my father's last message.

The pleasure, when it did come, did not last long. We were here. What good did it do me to know the hiding place of the precious gem? It meant nothing. If I had the chance now I would trade it for the safe return home of William and me.

We were going to die here. Perhaps two more marks on our rock. Three? Which one of us would die first? I could imagine the pirates on the *Reprise* betting on the outcome the way they had bet on the rats Herc had drowned. But they would never know who got it right. I hoped it would be me. To be here without William would be unbearable.

On the eighth day I saw a ship.

It was at the hottest time and we were in the rock shade. I had been playing my flute, playing a tune that William had said he liked. It was a sad song my mother used to sing about two children lost in the woods. There was a lonely wailing in the music and although William asked for it often I was not sure it was the right song for us now.

When I saw the sail I thought I was imagining it. It was far, far out in the sea, halfway between the island and the horizon. I dropped the flute and rubbed my eyes. The ship was still there.

"William!" I croaked. "Wake up. A ship!"

We ran and scrambled over the rocks and down onto the sand. William lit the kindling wood. He wrenched off his shirt, fanned the small flame and a thin trail of smoke began to rise.

I ran into the water, shouting as loudly as I could and waving my arms. "Here! We're here. Help us! Over here! Please!"

I screamed and waved even though the ship was

passing us by, its prow turning farther out to sea.

Our smoke sputtered and died.

I dropped to my knees in the water and sobbed. William ran to me and held me against him and whispered, "There, me love. There! Another ship'll come."

I buried my face against his chest. He smelled of smoke and sweat and he murmured words that I could barely hear. "Don't ye cry, me love. Ye're so brave. Ye're me brave girl."

I wasn't brave. I didn't know how I was going to be, for whatever time was left to us here on the island.

Chapter Nineteen

Our fire was only smoldering ash.

Our water was only a skin on the bottom of the rock. Sun had evaporated it even though William had spread his shirt across it, held up with stones, to make a shelter. We had no food now except the barnacles we scraped from the rocks.

There were twelve marks on our calendar, twelve days we'd been on Pox Island. Sometimes I thought of the other calendar and the fifteen scratches on it. Would we make it to fifteen?

I thought of the bones. We'd found them on the tenth day, or was it the eleventh? The days were running together.

"Animal bones," William had said as he scooped sand over them. I thought that there must have been wind one day that covered the bones where they lay, and that now they had resurfaced.

I knew they weren't from an animal. A long bone, a cradle-shaped one. I wept over the spot where William had recovered them, but I was dry crying. There wasn't enough water in my body to make tears.

Our energy had gone and we spent most of the days stretched out in whatever shade we could find or standing waist deep in the ocean trying to catch another fish. We had no luck.

William talked to me of ships and how he loved them and how, when we got off the island, peaceful ships would be his life. He drew a fleet of them for me in the sand... schooners, sloops with bowsprits as long as their hulls, two-masted brigantines, even a man o' war.

I spoke of the Burmese Sunrise and how my father had been so clever to hide it among the shells and pebbles and rocks in my mother's jar. I did not tell him of my presumptuous secret plans for selling it and using the money to start a life for us together when we escaped from Pox Island. I told him of my uneventful days before I became a pirate and of how I had longed for excitement.

With every day that passed, every hour, we grew

weaker.

I could still play my flute, and now and then I'd try for a happy tune to cheer us.

We never spoke of dying.

It was on the fourteenth night that we lay together, for comfort and perhaps for more. We understood, both of us, that the end was very near.

It was hard for me to understand that in spite of everything I still had feelings. That as we lay curled together, his chest warm against my back, I could still be overwhelmed by the emotions that welled up inside me. I knew so little about love, the kind between a man and a woman. I had been sheltered, my life tranquil and without passion. But I knew what this fullness, this need, meant. And I knew that William felt as I did.

We had never kissed. Once, early on, we had come close. But then William, not I, had pulled back.

"I'll not be takin' advantage of you, Catherine," he'd said. "But when we are through here, when we are safe, I will feel free to speak of my feelings."

We had touched, accidentally, a few times and when he touched me I seemed to turn to liquid. When he touched me I came alive.

Often I pondered how unfair it was that this new wonder had appeared to me when it was destined not to last.

Should I turn now to face him on this fourteenth night, as we lay so close together?

"They calls this 'spoonin', did ye know?" he asked, his whisper hoarse. "Like spoons nestled together in a drawer, fitting so perfectly."

"No," I murmured. "I did not know that." And I turned around.

His face was so close to mine.

"You told me that when this was over you would speak to me of your feelings. I don't want to wait for that. Tell me now, William."

In the light from a million stars I saw his smile. I ran my fingers through his yellow hair.

"I love ye," he whispered. "I know I'm not good enough for the likes of..."

I touched his lips. "You are good enough for anyone, anyone. I love you. I love you so much."

We kissed and there was such sweetness in the kiss. Fear was gone and there was only this newness.

Then there was more, a closeness that I had never imagined. There was no time for reason or for despairing thoughts of the ship that had sailed away and of the ships that might never come. We were together.

We slept, wrapped in each other's arms. Once I

wakened and looked up at the stars, and I thought only of love and of the miracle of it and I kissed his face before I slept again.

⚓

In the morning there was a shyness, almost an embarrassment between us.

"I watched you while you slept," William said.

"I watched *you!*"

"I'm goin' to gather more seaweed now to be ready for smoke when the next ship comes," he said. I nodded, trying to make my smile bright, not to let him see how futile I thought it to hope for another ship to come in time.

"No need for ye to stir yerself, love," he said. "Ye rest."

"It was a tiresome night," I said, mock seriously, and for a second our eyes met and we both laughed. I loved those blue, blue eyes of his, the color of the sea.

I watched him walk along the beach. He was so thin. The hairline scars that ran across his back were pale pink now, there forever. If we were to have a forever.

I took my flute and played, trying to recall some of my mother's favorites, searching my memory for songs of love.

My mother and my father came to me sometimes, stroking my hair, smiling and comforting me.

Red and Cook and Hopper and Herc slid in and out of my mind and I heard in the distance sea shanties and the crew of the *Reprisal* singing as they hauled on ropes or mended sails.

I was in a half doze, the flute hanging limply in my hand when I saw the ship.

Could I be dreaming? I didn't move for perhaps a minute and then I sprang to my feet. "William! William!" A scream exploded from my dry throat.

I scuttled, stumbling and gasping, to the water's edge.

William came, throwing down the few bits of seaweed, rushing to get the flint while I paddled into the ocean, waving with new energy, shouting again as I had shouted at the ship that had left us. I was still holding my flute and I waved it, too.

I recognized the ship as a brigantine, two-masted, with big, square sails that hung limp on this windless morning, and she was sailing on, sailing past us.

I choked on my despair.

And then I saw something. I saw the way the sun struck the top of the ship's mainmast and I knew the lookout was there, the sun glinting off his spyglass and I saw with sudden clarity the way the sun was glinting off my own flute.

I was suddenly alert.

I stood still in the water and moved my flute this way and that, seeing the shards of sun flash from it, slanting it toward the ship, up toward the lookout.

"Please," I whispered, "Please!"

I kept directing my shining flute, moving it in arcs, the flash of it touching the deck, the prow and always back to the crow's nest.

William was behind me and behind him was the thin wisp of smoke that rose from his seaweed fire.

Then, like a vision and the answer to prayers, I saw the ship change course, the sails filling weakly from a breath of wind, and it was coming, coming.

We held the flute, William's hand over mine, steadying our small beacon of light, calling for help.

The ship was heading toward Pox Island, the cloudiness of my tears making of it a shimmer of blue and white and a bowsprit that was a golden blur.

"Catherine!" William whispered. I felt his lips against my hair as we clung together, waist deep in the waters of Pox Island.

The two of us.

Waiting.

Eve Bunting grew up in Ireland—a country of storytellers—and came to California in 1958 with her husband and three small children. Her first book, an Irish folktale, was published in 1972. Since then she has written more than 250 books for children of all ages, from picture books to young adult novels, as well as non-fiction. She enjoys writing all types of stories for young readers, including those that address social issues.

Eve Bunting's books have won many awards and honors over the years, including the Golden Kite award from the Society of Children's Book Writers and Illustrators, the Edgar from the Mystery Writers of America, and awards from twenty-seven states voted on by children. She is a two-time winner of the California Young Reader Medal. In 2006 she won the first Arab American Book Award for *One Green Apple*, illustrated by Ted Lewin. Eve Bunting and her husband live in Pasadena, California. They now have six grandchildren.

An Interview with Eve Bunting

Author Eve Bunting (EB, below) talks with the editors of Sleeping Bear Press (SBP) about her experience writing The Pirate Captain's Daughter.

SBP: What made you decide to write a book about pirates?
EB: I've been interested in pirates ever since I was a little girl in Ireland and my father read *Treasure Island* to me. Sitting by a turf fire in our kitchen, rain falling outside, it was wonderful to picture the Caribbean, the sunshine, the trade winds . . . and the pirates.

I have always read books about pirates. I cherish my copy of *Treasure Island* with wonderful art by N.C. Wyeth. To me it not only evokes the days of the pirates but the days I spent listening to it and to my father's voice.

SBP: What research did you do for the book?
EB: When the thought came to me to write my very own pirate book I didn't have to look far past my imagination for facts. I have a library built up over the years by my family, who know of my fascination with Blackbeard and Captain Kidd and of course Grace O'Malley, the Irish pirate queen.

SBP: What inspired you to write this particular story?

EB: Perhaps it was Grace O'Malley who really inspired my story, since she set sail with her seafaring father when she was just a young girl and her bravery and skill are renowned. She even at one time went to call on Queen Elizabeth I and was well received.

There were other women who became pirates by the same ruse. Anne Bonny and Mary Reade were two of them. They dressed, fought, and swore like men. Once they even served, well disguised, on the same pirate ship. When they were captured they were sentenced together in Port Royal, Jamaica, and were both reprieved.

SBP: How did you create the character of Catherine?

EB: Because I write books for young people, my protagonist came full-blown as a teenager who "had always wanted to be a pirate." Catherine chopped off her hair, wore men's clothing and managed for quite a while to disguise her true sex so she could be part of her father's crew.

I had to do supplementary research of course when I began the book, so I haunted the Pasadena [California] public libraries. They know me well there and if I'm checking out a lot of pirate books they'll politely inquire, "Doing a pirate book next, Mrs. Bunting?" They are my friends and will gather books for me from all the branch libraries in town and beyond. I use the

Internet also but I do not entirely trust what I read and I find it helpful only when it puts me on track of some fact I may have already missed.

SBP: Can you tell your readers more about the pirate language?

EB: I had fun with the pirate dialogue which, on close examination, probably has a lot of the Irish in it. Many of the pirates were Irish, or English, so I think it all fit together. When I reread my final manuscript I smiled to recognize that some of the words coming out of the pirates' mouths had come out of my father's, "back in the day." If my father filled a glass of water too full and it sloshed on the tablecloth he'd mutter "It was lippin' laggin'," meaning full to the top. Then he might conclude with a hearty "Dogblast!" He certainly would have been surprised if he'd heard a pirate on the *Reprisal* speaking the way he did.

SBP: Are there modern-day pirates?

EB: Unfortunately there are still pirates today plying their trade. They troll the sea and plunder ships, usually cargo vessels and tankers carrying oil. Most of the "hot spots" are off the coast of Somalia in the Indian Ocean. Instead of cannons or cutlasses they carry machine guns and automatic rifles. Instead of sails they use motorboats or fishing craft fitted with powerful engines. There is not much gold or many jewels being carried in today's cargo vessels but the pirates will steal whatever they can find—computers, laptops, cell phones, iPods, clothing. In 2005 two heavily armed pirate boats even attacked a cruise ship and tried unsuccessfully to board it. AARG!

"Bad cess to them!" my father would have said.

SBP: Did you enjoy writing *The Pirate Captain's Daughter*?
EB: I so much enjoyed writing this novel. I loved Catherine and William and did not want to let go of them. But all good things must come to an end.

If I do write another pirate story I will have a new book to aid me in my research.

I will have *The Pirate Captain's Daughter*.

A Note to Readers

If you participate in a reading group or book club and want to discuss The Pirate Captain's Daughter, *here are some questions to get you started:*

1. *The Pirate Captain's Daughter* is a historical novel. Are there any clues in the book that give you an indication of when it took place? [Hint: One clue has to do with a book!]

2. Would you want to have lived during the period in history that *The Pirate Captain's Daughter* takes place? What would you like about it? What would you miss from the present day?

3. If you lived during the time the book took place, do you think you could be a pirate? Could you live under the conditions that Catherine lived?

4. In the book, William finds out Catherine's secret. "I'll not be telling," he says to Catherine, and she trusts him. Are there people in your life who you would trust with a big secret? Are you good at keeping secrets?

5. *The Pirate Captain's Daughter* is a historical novel, a mystery, an adventure story, and a romance. Which are your favorite aspects of the story? What kind of story would *you* want to write?

These are just a few of the many questions that you can think of and try to answer yourself or in discussion with a group of your friends or classmates.